Shine Your Light

Well-rounded, Educational e-book for preschoolers about wisdom, respecting teachers, parents, and elders. Teenagers, with practical activities and reflections included to deepen understanding and foster respect:

KASIMWE S BONGERIZE

Dedication

To the world, to the education system, parents, young children, adults, and elders— May this light serve as a guiding beacon for all.

And above all, to my children and the next generation to come—

May your luminous spirits shine brightly, leading us into a new era of love, wisdom, and awakening.

Acknowledgment

I dedicate deep gratitude to everyone who holds the vision of awakening and healing for humanity.

To the educators, parents, guardians, and elders—your dedication and love nurture the seeds of wisdom and respect in every heart.

To the children and young adults—your radiant light is the hope and future of our planet. And to my own children and the children of the world—may your luminous spirits continue to inspire and transform.

Thank you for your guidance, support, and unwavering belief in the power of love and awakening. This work is a reflection of your collective light and purpose.

Contents

Basic Concept of Respect in a Simple

Section 1: Understanding Respect

What is Respect?

Respect is one of the most important values a child can learn. It means treating others with kindness, listening to them, and understanding their feelings. When we respect someone, we

show them that we care about them and appreciate who they are. For preschoolers, respect can be taught in simple ways, like using polite words, listening when someone is talking, and being

gentle with friends and family.

Why We Listen to Parents and Teachers

Parents and teachers help children grow, learn, and stay safe. They teach important lessons, guide children through challenges, and make sure they are cared for. When kids listen to their parents and teachers, they learn new things faster and understand the right way to behave. Respecting their advice means following instructions, asking for help when needed, and appreciating the wisdom they share.

Using Kind Words

Words have power, and using kind words can make others feel happy and valued. Teaching

preschoolers to say **"please," "thank you," "excuse me," and "I'm sorry"** helps them express respect in their daily interactions. When children learn to speak politely, they create positive

relationships with family, teachers, and friends. Encouraging kids to use kind words even when they feel upset teaches them how to communicate with respect.

Helping Hands

One way to show respect is by being helpful. Whether it's picking up toys, setting the table, or helping a friend who dropped something, small acts of kindness make a big difference. Teaching preschoolers that helping others shows care and appreciation encourages them to be thoughtful. A simple phrase like **"We help because we care"** can reinforce the idea that helping is a way to show respect.

Taking Turns and Sharing

Sharing is an important way to respect others. Whether it's sharing toys, books, or snacks, it teaches children that others' needs and feelings matter too. Taking turns helps children practice patience and understand fairness. When kids learn to share and wait their turn, they build strong friendships and create a happier environment at home and school.

Respecting Personal Space

Everyone has a personal space, and respecting it is part of showing kindness. Teaching preschoolers to keep their hands to themselves, ask before hugging, and avoid grabbing toys

Basic Concept of Respect in a Simple

from others helps them understand boundaries. Simple phrases like **"Hands to yourself"** or **"Ask before you touch"** can help reinforce this lesson. Respecting personal space helps children feel safe and comfortable around others.

Listening When Someone is Speaking

Good listening is a key part of respect. When someone talks, it's important to pay attention, make eye contact, and not interrupt. Teaching preschoolers to listen before they speak helps them understand the importance of conversations. A fun way to practice this is by playing **"Listening Games,"** where kids have to repeat back what they heard. This skill will help them in school, at home, and with friends.

Using Gentle Hands and Voices

Respect isn't just about words—it's also about actions. Using gentle hands means not hitting, pushing, or grabbing. A gentle voice means speaking in a calm and friendly tone instead of yelling or whining. Children can learn that being gentle makes others feel safe and happy.

Role-playing different situations where they practice using gentle hands and voices can help them build this habit.

Respecting Differences

People come from different backgrounds, have different

likes and dislikes, and may look different. Teaching children to respect these differences helps them develop kindness and an open mind. Preschoolers can learn that it's okay for someone to have a different favorite color, a different way of talking, or a different type of food they enjoy. Books and stories about diversity can help children understand the beauty of respecting everyone.

Practicing Respect Every Day

Respect is something we show every day through small actions. From saying "good morning" to greeting teachers with a smile, every act of kindness adds up. Parents and teachers can encourage kids to practice respect by using positive reinforcement, like praising respectful behavior.

Making respect a daily habit helps preschoolers grow into kind, thoughtful, and well-mannered individuals.

Section 2: Respecting Parents & Family

1. Mom and Dad Take Care of Me

Parents work hard to provide food, shelter, and love for their children. They wake up early to prepare meals, go to work to support the family, and make sure their children are safe and happy. Teaching preschoolers to appreciate their parents' efforts helps them understand why respect is important. Simple actions like saying "thank you" after a meal or giving a hug show appreciation for all that parents do.

Helping at Home

Children can show respect by helping at home with small tasks. Simple chores, like putting away toys, setting the table, or helping to water plants, teach responsibility and teamwork. When preschoolers help around the house, they learn that families work together to keep their home clean and organized. Parents can encourage this by making chores fun and praising their child's efforts.

Respecting Our Grandparents

Grandparents have many stories and life lessons to share. They often have wisdom that comes from years of experience. Teaching preschoolers to respect and listen to their grandparents helps strengthen family bonds. Simple ways to show respect include greeting grandparents with a smile, listening to their stories, and offering to help them with small tasks. Respecting elders

means valuing their presence and treating them with kindness.

Saying "I Love You" with Actions

Words are important, but actions speak louder. Preschoolers can express love and respect for their parents and family members through kind gestures. Giving a big hug, drawing a picture as a gift, or offering to help are all ways to say "I love you." Parents can teach children that love is not just something we say, but something we show through caring actions every day.

Listening Without Interrupting

When parents or family members are talking, it's important to listen without interrupting. Teaching preschoolers to wait for their turn to speak helps them learn patience and respect.

Parents can practice this by modeling good listening behavior—making eye contact and giving their full attention. A simple rule like **"One person speaks at a time"** helps children understand that listening is an important part of communication.

Respecting Family Rules

Every family has rules that help things run smoothly. Whether it's bedtime routines, meal manners, or screen time limits, following family rules shows respect. When children understand that laws exist to keep them safe and happy, they are more likely to follow them. Parents can reinforce this by simply explaining rules and celebrating when their child makes good choices.

Using Polite Words at Home

Respect starts at home, and using polite words with family members is a great way to practice. Teaching children to say "please," "thank you," "excuse me," and "sorry" when needed creates a positive and loving atmosphere. Parents can encourage this by using polite words themselves, making it a habit that children naturally follow.

Respecting Siblings and Family Members

Brothers, sisters, and other family members deserve respect, too. Teaching preschoolers to share, take turns, and use kind words with their siblings helps create a peaceful home. If disagreements happen, parents can guide their children in resolving conflicts calmly. Learning to respect family members prepares children for positive relationships outside the house as well.

Expressing Gratitude for Family

Being thankful for family is an important part of respect. Parents can teach preschoolers to say "thank you" for small things, like making a meal or giving a ride to school. Making gratitude a daily habit helps children appreciate their family and recognize all the love and care they receive.

Respecting Family Time

Family time is special, and showing respect means being present and engaged. Whether it's during mealtime, story time, or family outings, putting away distractions and enjoying the moment shows appreciation. Teaching preschoolers to focus on family activities helps them understand that spending time together is valuable and should be treated with respect.

Section 3: Respecting Teachers & School Rules

1. Why Teachers Are Special

Teachers play an important role in helping children learn and grow. They spend time preparing lessons, answering questions, and making sure every child gets the support they need. Respecting teachers means listening to them, following their instructions, and appreciating their hard work. When children understand that teachers are there to help them, they are more likely to respect and learn from them.

Listening in Class

Listening carefully in class is a way to show respect to teachers and classmates. When a teacher is talking, students should stay quiet, make eye contact, and focus on what is being taught.

Paying attention helps children learn better and makes the classroom a peaceful place where everyone can succeed. Parents can reinforce this at home by practicing listening games and modeling good listening behavior.

Raising Your Hand

One important classroom rule is raising a hand before speaking. This helps keep order and ensures that everyone gets a chance to share their thoughts. Teaching preschoolers to wait their turn to talk helps them develop patience and good manners. It also shows respect for their teacher and classmates by allowing everyone to participate without interruptions.

Being Kind to Classmates

Respecting teachers also means respecting classmates. Using kind words, sharing, and helping friends are ways to create a positive learning environment. When children are kind to each other, it makes the classroom a happy place for everyone. Teaching kids to include others in games and activities helps build strong friendships and prevents bullying.

Taking Care of School Property

Books, chairs, desks, and playground equipment are shared by all students, so taking care of them is important. Teaching children to respect school supplies by using them gently and putting them away properly helps maintain a clean and organized classroom. A simple rule like **"If you take it out, put it back"** can remind preschoolers to be responsible with school materials.

Following Classroom Rules

Classroom rules are made to keep students safe and help everyone learn better. Rules like **"no running inside," "use an inside voice," and "clean up after yourself"** are there to make sure the classroom stays a happy place. Teaching preschoolers to follow rules, even when they don't feel like it, helps them understand discipline and the importance of respecting their teacher's guidance.

Saying "Good Morning" and "Thank You"

Greeting the teacher and saying "thank you" at the end of the day is a simple way to show respect. When students start the day with a polite **"Good morning, teacher!"** it sets a positive tone. At the end of the day, saying "thank you for teaching me" reminds children to appreciate their teacher's efforts. Parents can encourage this by practicing polite greetings and thank-yous at home.

Keeping Hands and Feet to Yourself

Respecting personal space is an important part of classroom behavior. Pushing, grabbing, or hitting is not respectful and can make others feel unsafe. Teaching children to **"use gentle hands"** and **"keep hands and feet to yourself"** helps prevent conflicts and encourages kindness. Role-playing different scenarios can help preschoolers practice self-control and respectful behavior.

Asking for Help Nicely

Sometimes, children need help with a task or a question. Teaching preschoolers to ask for help politely—using words like **"Excuse me, teacher"** or **"May I have help, please?"**—shows good manners and respect. Encouraging children to express their needs respectfully helps them communicate better and build positive relationships with their teachers.

Respecting Different Learning Styles

Every child learns in their own way, and some classmates may need more time or different methods to understand a lesson. Teaching preschoolers to be patient and supportive of their peers helps create a caring classroom environment. Encouraging kids to celebrate their classmates' Successes instead of comparing themselves fosters respect and teamwork in learning.

Section 4: Wisdom & Making Good Choices

1. Making Smart Choices

Wisdom is about making smart choices every day. Preschoolers may not always understand what is right or wrong, but they can learn by thinking before acting. A smart choice means doing what is safe, kind, and helpful. Parents and teachers can help children by asking questions like, **"Is this a good choice?"** or **"What might happen if you do this?"** to guide their decision-making.

Learning from Mistakes

Everyone makes mistakes, and that's okay! What's important is learning from them. If a child spills their drink, instead of getting upset, they can learn to clean it up. If they forget to share, they can remember to do better next time. Teaching preschoolers that mistakes help us grow encourages them to keep trying and not be afraid of learning new things.

Being Honest and Truthful

Honesty is an important part of being wise. When children tell the truth, they build trust with their parents, teachers, and friends. Even if they make a mistake, being honest shows they are responsible. Parents can encourage honesty by praising their child when they tell the truth, saying things like, **"I'm proud of you for being honest."**

Shine Your Light

Patience is a Superpower

Preschoolers often want things **right now**, but wisdom means understanding that sometimes we need to wait. Whether it's waiting for a turn on the slide or for food to be ready, patience helps children stay calm and happy. Teaching kids simple breathing exercises or singing a song while waiting can make patience easier to practice.

Thinking Before Speaking

Words are powerful, and wise children learn to think before they speak. If they feel upset, they should pause and ask, **"Is this a kind thing to say?"** Instead of yelling, they can learn to use gentle words to express feelings. Parents can help by modeling kind speech and teaching children how to apologize when they say something hurtful.

Choosing Friends Wisely

Friends influence how we act, so choosing kind and respectful friends is important. Preschoolers should learn to play with children who are nice, share, and make them feel happy. Parents and teachers can ask questions like, **"Does your friend make good choices?"** to help children think about the friends they spend time with.

Listening to Advice

Wise children listen to parents, teachers, and elders because they have experience and knowledge. When children follow good advice, they avoid trouble and learn new things.

Parents can share simple stories about times they followed good advice and how it helped them. Encouraging kids to ask for help when unsure teaches them that listening is an important skill.

Staying Calm When Things Go Wrong

Life doesn't always go as planned, and sometimes things don't go our way. Instead of crying or getting angry, wise children learn to stay calm. Deep breaths, counting to five, or taking a break can help preschoolers handle disappointment. Teaching them to say, **"It's okay, I'll try again!"** helps build resilience.

A Thankful Heart is a Happy Heart

Gratitude is a big part of wisdom. When children appreciate what they have, they feel happier. Simple habits like saying **"thank you"** for food, toys, or a fun day teach children to focus on the good things in life. Parents can encourage gratitude by asking, **"What was your favorite part of today?"** before bedtime.

Learning Every Day

Wise children know that learning never stops. Every day is a chance to grow, whether it's learning a new word, trying a new food, or making a new friend. Encouraging curiosity and a love for learning helps preschoolers develop a wise and open-minded attitude that will benefit them for life.

Section 5: Being Kind & Helping Others

1.   What Does It Mean to Be Kind?

Kindness is one of the most important values a child can learn. Being kind means using gentle words, helping others, and treating people with care. When children understand that kindness makes the world a better place, they are more likely to practice it daily. Parents and teachers can reinforce kindness by praising good behavior and setting an example.

Using Kind Words

Words have the power to make someone feel happy or sad. Teaching preschoolers to say **"please," "thank you," "sorry,"** and **"excuse me"** helps them communicate respectfully. Encouraging them to compliment others, such as saying, **"I like your drawing!"** or **"You did a great job!"**, helps build confidence and positive relationships.

Sharing With Friends and Family

Sharing is a way to show kindness and care for others. Whether it's a toy, a snack, or crayons, sharing teaches children that giving can bring joy. Preschoolers can practice sharing by playing games that involve taking turns or working together. Parents can encourage this by saying, **"Sharing makes everyone happy!"**

Helping at Home

Even small hands can help in big ways! Teaching children to help at home builds responsibility and shows appreciation for their family. Simple tasks like putting away toys, setting the table, or helping a sibling teach the value of teamwork. When children realize that helping makes life easier for everyone, they are more likely to develop a habit of kindness.

Helping Friends at School

Kindness doesn't stop at home—it continues in school too! Helping a friend who dropped their books, comforting someone who is sad, or letting a friend borrow a toy are ways to be kind in the classroom. Teachers can encourage this by creating a **"kindness chart"** where children can see how their good deeds make a difference.

Being Kind to Animals

Kindness isn't just for people—it's for animals too! Teaching children to be gentle with pets, not to hurt insects, and to respect nature helps them develop empathy for all living things. Parents can model this behavior by showing how to pet animals gently and explaining that animals have feelings, too.

Listening When Someone Talks

Listening is a great way to show kindness and respect. When someone is speaking, looking at them and not interrupting shows that we care about their words. Teaching preschoolers to listen helps them build strong friendships and shows them that everyone's thoughts and feelings matter.

Saying Sorry When We Hurt Someone

Sometimes, we make mistakes and accidentally hurt someone's feelings. Teaching children to say **"I'm sorry"** when they do something wrong helps them take responsibility for their actions. It also teaches them that apologizing can help fix problems and make others feel better. Parents can encourage this by saying, **"Saying sorry shows you care."**

Spreading Smiles and Happiness

A simple smile can brighten someone's day! Teaching children that small acts of kindness—like smiling, giving a high-five, or saying a kind word—can make others happy is an important lesson. Parents and teachers can make this a fun challenge by encouraging kids to **"make someone smile every day!"**

Kindness Makes the World Better

When children understand that every kind action makes the world a happier place, they feel encouraged to continue being kind. Reading stories about kindness, watching acts of kindness in real life, and celebrating their own good deeds help reinforce this lesson. A world filled with kindness starts with teaching children that **every act of kindness, no matter how small, makes a big difference!**

Section 6: Being Honest & Telling the Truth

1.   What Does It Mean to Be Honest?

Honesty means telling the truth, even when it's hard. It also means being fair, not taking things that don't belong to us, and doing what is right. Teaching preschoolers about honesty helps them build strong relationships with their family, friends, and teachers. Parents can start by explaining that honesty is about being **trustworthy** and **doing the right thing** even when no one is watching.

Why Telling the Truth is Important

When we tell the truth, people know they can trust us. If we lie, others may feel hurt or disappointed. Teaching children that **"honesty makes people happy, and lying makes people sad"** helps them understand why truthfulness is important. Parents can use stories or real-life examples to show how honesty builds trust.

The Problem with Lying

Sometimes, children may be tempted to lie to avoid getting into trouble. However, lying often makes things worse. When someone lies, they have to keep making up more stories, which can become confusing and stressful. Teaching children that **"a small lie can turn into a big problem"** helps them understand that telling the truth is always the best choice.

Admitting Mistakes and Saying Sorry

Everyone makes mistakes, and that's okay! What matters is admitting them. If a child spills their juice or forgets to put away their toys, they should feel safe to say, **"I made a mistake, and I'm sorry."** Parents and teachers can encourage honesty by **not punishing children harshly** when they tell the truth. Instead, they should praise them for being honest and help them fix the mistake.

Honesty in Everyday Life

Being honest is not just about telling the truth; it's also about being fair. For example, if a child finds a toy that doesn't belong to them, being honest means returning it to the owner. If they accidentally break something, they should let someone know instead of hiding it. These small moments help children practice honesty in their daily lives.

Honesty and Feelings

Sometimes, honesty is about kindly expressing our feelings. If a child doesn't like something, they can be honest without being rude. Instead of saying, **"I don't like your drawing!"**, they can say, "I like the colors you used, but I like drawing animals more."

Teaching children to be honest **without hurting others' feelings** helps them communicate better.

The Reward of Being Honest

When we are honest, people respect and trust us more. If children always tell the truth, their parents, teachers, and friends will know that they can believe what they say. Children can also feel proud of themselves when they tell the truth because they are doing the right thing.

How to Make Honesty a Habit

Honesty is something we practice every day. Parents and teachers can help by **leading by example**—if a child sees adults being honest, they will learn to do the same. Fun activities like storytelling, role-playing, and praising honesty can encourage children to be truthful.

What to Do If Someone Lies

If a child notices someone else lying, they should understand that everyone makes mistakes. Instead of being angry, they can encourage their friend or sibling to tell the truth. Parents can teach children to say things like, **"It's okay to tell the truth. I will still be your friend."** This creates a supportive environment where honesty is encouraged.

Honesty Makes Us Better People

Being honest helps children grow into **kind, responsible, and trustworthy** people. It strengthens relationships and makes life easier. When preschoolers understand that honesty **helps them feel good inside**, they are more likely to choose truthfulness every time.

Section 7: Being Responsible & Doing Your Best

1. What Does It Mean to Be Responsible?

Responsibility means taking care of things and making good choices. When children are responsible, they complete their tasks, take care of their belongings, and help others. Learning responsibility at a young age allows preschoolers to grow into dependable and trustworthy people. Parents and teachers can encourage responsibility by assigning small tasks and praising children when they follow through.

Taking Care of Personal Belongings

A responsible child knows how to take care of their toys, clothes, and school supplies. Instead of leaving toys on the floor, they put them away after playing. Instead of dropping their jacket anywhere, they hang it up. Teaching children to take care of their things helps them appreciate what they have and keeps their space clean. A simple rule like **"Put it back where it belongs"** helps reinforce responsibility.

Cleaning Up After Yourself

Preschoolers should learn that cleaning up after themselves is an important part of responsibility. Whether it's putting their dishes in the sink after eating or picking up toys after playtime, taking care of their mess shows they are growing up. Parents can make this fun by setting a **"clean-up song"** or a **"race to tidy up"** game to encourage children to take responsibility for their spaces.

Completing Small Tasks

Even young children can handle simple responsibilities like feeding a pet, watering plants, or putting away their shoes. Completing small tasks helps preschoolers feel proud of themselves. When parents or teachers say, **"Wow! You did that all by yourself!"**, it encourages children to keep trying and take on more responsibilities.

Following Rules and Routines

Following rules at home and school is part of being responsible. Rules keep everyone safe and happy. For example, washing hands before eating, looking both ways before crossing the street, and saying **"please"** and **"thank you"** are all responsibilities that help children learn self-discipline. When children understand that rules are there to help them, they become more willing to follow them.

Taking Responsibility for Actions

Sometimes, children make mistakes, like spilling a drink or forgetting to share. Instead of blaming others, responsible children admit what they did and try to fix it. Teaching children to say, **"I'm sorry, I'll clean it up"** or **"Next time, I will remember"** helps them learn from their actions. Parents can praise honesty and effort, saying, **"It's okay to make mistakes as long as we learn from them."**

Shine Your Light

Doing Your Best in Everything

Being responsible also means trying your best, even when something is difficult. Whether it's coloring a picture, putting on shoes, or learning a new word, children should be encouraged to **keep trying** instead of giving up. Parents and teachers can remind them, **"You don't have to be perfect- just do your best!"** This helps children develop a growth mindset and confidence in their abilities.

Helping Others When You Can

Responsible children don't just take care of themselves- they also help others. Whether it's assisting a younger sibling, holding the door for someone, or helping a friend pick up toys, small acts of kindness show responsibility. Teaching preschoolers that helping others **makes the world a better place** encourages them to be caring and thoughtful.

Being Responsible with Time

Learning how to **use time wisely** is an important responsibility. Children should understand when it's time to play, eat, sleep, and learn. Creating a simple schedule with pictures or a daily routine chart can help preschoolers remember their responsibilities. When children follow a routine, they feel more independent and in control of their day.

Responsibility Helps Us Grow

When preschoolers learn to be responsible, they feel proud,

confident, and capable. Being accountable means that others can trust them, and they can trust themselves to handle tasks and challenges. Responsibility helps children grow into **kind, hardworking, and reliable** individuals. Parents and teachers can remind children that every time they **make a good choice, help someone, or finish a task**, they are learning an important skill for life.

Section 8: Respecting Teachers, Parents, and Elders

1. What Does Respect Mean?

Respect means treating others with kindness, listening to them, and showing appreciation for their help and guidance. When children respect their teachers, parents, and elders, they build strong relationships and learn valuable lessons. Respect can be shown in many ways, like using polite words, following rules, and being a good listener.

Using Polite Words

Words like **"please," "thank you," "excuse me,"** and **"sorry"** show respect. Teaching preschoolers to use these words helps them understand that good manners make others feel valued. Parents and teachers can encourage respect by modeling these words in daily conversations, such as saying, **"Thank you for helping me!"** when a child does a small task.

Listening When Someone Speaks

Listening is an important way to show respect. When a teacher, parent, or elder is speaking, children should learn to stop what they are doing, look at the person, and pay attention. This shows that they care about what is being said. Parents can practice this by saying, **"Let's take turns talking. Now it's your turn to listen!"**

Basic Concept of Respect in a Simple

Following Rules at Home and School

Rules help keep everyone safe and happy. Respecting parents and teachers means listening to their instructions and following the rules they set. Simple rules like washing hands before eating, picking up toys after playing, and waiting for a turn in class help children learn self-discipline.

When children understand that rules are made to help them, they are more likely to follow them happily.

Helping Parents, Teachers, and Elders

Another way to show respect is by helping without being asked. Preschoolers can show respect to parents by cleaning up their toys, helping set the table, or giving a big hug. In school, they can help their teacher by putting away books or sharing with a friend. Small acts of kindness show appreciation and make adults feel loved.

Speaking in a Kind and Gentle Way

Children should learn to speak to adults with a kind and gentle voice. Yelling, whining, or using rude words is disrespectful. Teaching children to say, **"Can I have help, please?"** instead of demanding, **"I want this now!"** helps them communicate respectfully. Parents and teachers can remind children, **"Let's use our kind voices."**

Understanding That Elders Have Wisdom

Grandparents, teachers, and older adults have many experiences and stories to share. Teaching children to respect their wisdom means listening to their advice and valuing their lessons. Parents can tell children, **"Grandma has lived for many years and knows a lot! Let's listen to her stories."** This helps preschoolers understand that elders have important knowledge to share.

Waiting Patiently and Taking Turns

Respecting adults means understanding that sometimes children need to wait their turn to speak or receive attention. If a teacher is talking to another student, a child should wait quietly instead of interrupting. At home, if a parent is on the phone, children should wait patiently. Teaching children to say, **"Excuse me"** before speaking helps them learn to be respectful.

Showing Appreciation for Teachers and Parents

Teachers, parents, and elders do a lot to help children learn and grow. Saying **"thank you"** or drawing a picture for a teacher is a small way to show appreciation. Parents can encourage this by asking, **"What do you love about your teacher?"** or **"How can we show Grandma that we appreciate her?"** Gratitude helps children recognize the kindness they receive.

Basic Concept of Respect in a Simple

Respect Makes Everyone Happy

When children learn to respect their parents, teachers, and elders, they create a happy and caring environment. Respect helps build trust, friendship, and love between children and adults.

Teaching preschoolers that **"respect makes the world a better place"** encourages them to practice it every day, helping them grow into kind and thoughtful individuals.

Section 9: Being a Good Friend & Treating Others Kindly

1. What Does It Mean to Be a Good Friend?

Being a good friend means being kind, sharing, helping others, and treating them with respect. Friends make us happy, play with us, and support us when we feel sad. Teaching preschoolers how to be good friends helps them build strong relationships and develop social skills that will help them throughout life.

Sharing and Taking Turns

One of the most important parts of friendship is sharing. Whether it's toys, crayons, or a favorite snack, sharing shows kindness and helps friends feel included. Preschoolers should also learn to take turns, like letting a friend go first on the slide or using a toy for a little while before passing it to someone else. Parents and teachers can encourage sharing by saying, **"Let's take turns so everyone has fun!"**

Using Kind Words

Words have the power to make people feel happy or sad. Teaching children to use kind words ike **"please," "thank you," "I like your drawing,"** or **"You're a great friend!"** helps create a positive and friendly environment. If a child accidentally hurts someone's feelings, they should learn to say, **"I'm sorry, I didn't mean to hurt you."** This helps preschoolers understand that

Words should be used to build friendships, not to hurt others.

Helping Friends When They Need It

A good friend helps others when they need support. If a friend falls on the playground, a kind child helps them up. If a friend is sad, a kind child asks, **"Are you okay?"** and tries to make them feel better. Parents can teach their children to notice when someone needs help and say,

"Helping others makes us feel good inside, too!"

Listening and Taking Turns to Talk

Friendship isn't just about talking- it's also about listening. When a friend is speaking, a good listener looks at them, waits for them to finish, and responds kindly. Teaching preschoolers not to interrupt and to **"listen with their ears and their hearts"** helps them build strong friendships.

Including Everyone in Play

Sometimes, children may feel left out when others don't include them in games. Teaching preschoolers to invite others to play by saying, **"Do you want to join us?"** helps everyone feel welcome. Parents and teachers can remind children that **"everyone deserves to have fun"** and encourage them to be inclusive.

Shine Your Light

Solving Problems Peacefully

Disagreements happen in friendships, but good friends solve problems **without yelling, hitting, or being mean**. Teaching children to use words like **"Let's take turns," "Can we find a way to share?"** or **"I didn't like that, but let's be friends again"** helps them positively resolve conflicts. Parents can guide children by asking, **"How can we fix this problem together?"**

Respecting Differences in Friends

Friends may have different interests, favorite colors, or ways of doing things. Teaching preschoolers that **"it's okay to be different"** helps them appreciate diversity. If a friend likes soccer but another friend likes drawing, they can take turns playing each other's favorite activities. Learning that differences make friendships more fun helps children be more accepting.

Standing Up for Friends

A good friend stands up for others when they see something unfair happening. If a child notices a friend being left out, they can invite them to play. If a friend is feeling sad, they can offer comfort. Parents and teachers can teach children to say, **"It's not nice to leave someone out. Let's all play together!"** to encourage kindness and inclusion.

Friendship Makes Life Better

Being a good friend brings happiness to everyone. When

children learn to treat others with kindness, share, help, and listen, they create strong and lasting friendships. Teaching preschoolers that **"friendship is about making others happy and feeling happy too"** encourages them to practice kindness every day. A world full of good friends is a world filled with joy!

Section 10: Saying Sorry & Learning from Mistakes

1. Everyone Makes Mistakes

Mistakes are a natural part of growing up. Sometimes, children might spill their juice, break a toy, or forget to share. It's important to teach preschoolers that making mistakes is okay because mistakes help us learn. Instead of feeling bad about a mistake, they should focus on how to fix it and do better next time.

What Does It Mean to Say Sorry?

Saying **"I'm sorry"** is a way to show that we care about other people's feelings. When we hurt someone, even by accident, apologizing helps make things better. A sincere apology means we understand what went wrong and want to fix it. Parents and teachers can encourage children by saying, **"When we say sorry, we show that we are kind and responsible."**

When Should We Say Sorry?

Children should learn that we say sorry when we hurt someone's feelings, make a mistake, or do something wrong. If they take a toy from a friend, they should apologize and give it back. If they bump into someone by accident, a simple **"Oops! I'm sorry!"** can make the other person feel better. Understanding when to say sorry helps children build good relationships.

Basic Concept of Respect in a Simple

Saying Sorry with Actions

Apologies should be more than just words. If a child knocks over a friend's blocks, they can say **"I'm sorry"** and then help rebuild the tower. If they forget to share, they can say, **"Sorry, let's play together now."** Teaching children that actions matter just as much as words helps them become truly kind and responsible.

Learning from Mistakes

Every mistake is a chance to learn something new. If a child forgets to clean up their toys, they can learn to put them away next time. If they don't listen to their teacher and miss an instruction, they can learn to pay better attention. Teaching preschoolers that **"mistakes help us grow"** makes them feel more confident in trying again.

Being Patient with Ourselves and Others

Sometimes, children get upset when they make mistakes, but they should learn to be kind to themselves. Saying, **"It's okay, I'll do better next time,"** helps build a positive attitude. Parents and teachers can also show patience by reassuring children, **"Nobody is perfect. We all make mistakes and learn from them."**

Accepting Apologies from Others

Just like we say sorry when we hurt someone, we should also forgive others when they apologize to us. If a friend says, **"I'm sorry for not sharing"**, children should learn to respond with **"It's okay, let's play together now!"** Learning to forgive helps build strong friendships and prevents small problems from becoming big ones.

The Power of Trying Again

When children learn from their mistakes, they get better and stronger. If they struggle to tie their shoes, they should keep practicing until they get it right. If they forget to say **"please"** and **"thank you"**, they can remember next time. Teaching preschoolers that **"practice makes progress"** encourages them to keep trying, no matter what.

Making Good Choices

Saying sorry is important, but it's even better to **try not to repeat the same mistake**. If a child pushes a friend, they should not only say sorry but also remember to use gentle hands next time. Helping children think about better choices, like using words instead of actions when upset, helps them become more responsible.

Apologies Make the World Kinder

Saying sorry and learning from mistakes help children become kinder, more understanding people. When everyone takes responsibility for their actions and tries to improve, friendships grow stronger, and the world becomes a better place. Teaching preschoolers that **"a heartfelt sorry and a lesson learned make everything better"** helps them build a positive and caring attitude for life.

Section 11: Listening and Following Instructions

1. Why Listening Is Important

Listening is one of the most important skills a child can learn. When children listen carefully, they understand what to do, follow rules, and show respect to teachers, parents, and friends.

Good listening helps children learn new things and stay safe in different situations. Teaching preschoolers that **"listening helps us understand and be understood"** encourages them to pay attention.

How to Be a Good Listener

Good listening means looking at the person speaking, staying quiet, and focusing on their words. Preschoolers should be taught to **"listen with their ears, eyes, and heart."** This means using their ears to hear, their eyes to look at the speaker, and their heart to care about what is being said. Practicing this skill with simple games like **"Simon Says"** can help children develop better listening habits.

Following Simple Instructions

Following instructions is an important part of listening. Instructions help children know what to do, like **"Put your toys away"** or **"Wash your hands before eating."** When children follow directions, they learn responsibility and develop self-control. Parents and teachers can make it fun by giving small challenges, like **"Can you hop to the door and then clap your hands?"**

Paying Attention in School and at Home

In school, children need to listen to their teachers to learn new things. If they don't pay attention, they might miss important lessons. At home, listening helps children understand family rules and expectations. A good way to encourage listening is by reminding children, **"When we listen, we learn and grow!"**

Why Interrupting Is Not Okay

Interrupting while someone is talking is not respectful. Teaching preschoolers to wait for their turn to speak helps them become patient and considerate. A simple trick is telling them, **"Put your hand on my arm if you need to say something, and I'll know you're waiting."** This helps them feel heard while still being respectful.

Listening for Safety

Listening carefully is especially important for safety. If a parent or teacher says **"Stop!"**, children need to hear right away to avoid danger. Teaching preschoolers that listening can **keep them safe on the road, in the playground, and at home** helps them understand why paying attention is so important.

Making Listening Fun

Listening can be taught through fun activities like storytelling, music, and interactive games. **"Storytime listening"** encourages children to focus on words and understand the meaning behind them. Playing **"repeat after me"** or listening to songs with actions helps develop listening skills in a fun way.

The Benefits of Following Instructions

When children follow instructions, they **complete tasks correctly, learn faster, and make fewer mistakes**. Whether it's following a recipe with a parent or listening to a teacher explain a game, understanding instructions helps them succeed. Encouraging children by saying, **"Good listening helps you do great things!"** makes them feel proud of their efforts.

What Happens When We Don't Listen?

When children don't listen, they may forget important things, make mistakes, or even upset others. If a child doesn't listen when a teacher gives directions, they might struggle with their activity. Teaching children that **"not listening can make things harder, but listening makes things easier"** helps them understand why paying attention is important.

Shine Your Light

Listening Makes Everyone Happy

When children listen, they build better friendships, learn more, and show respect to those around them. Parents and teachers should praise good listening by saying, **"I love how you listened so carefully! Great job!"** Positive reinforcement helps children feel motivated to listen more often, making them better learners and more respectful individuals.

Section 12: Being Honest & Telling the Truth

1. What Does It Mean to Be Honest?

Honesty means always telling the truth and doing the right thing, even when no one is watching. It's about being truthful in words and actions. When children learn to be honest, they build trust with their parents, teachers, and friends. Teaching preschoolers that **"honesty means telling the truth and being fair"** helps them understand why it's important.

Why Is Telling the Truth Important?

Telling the truth helps people trust and believe in us. When we are honest, others know they can count on us. If a child accidentally breaks something and tells the truth about it, their parents will appreciate their honesty. Teaching children that **"it's always better to tell the truth than to hide a mistake"** helps them develop integrity.

Honesty Helps Us Feel Good Inside

When we tell the truth, we feel proud of ourselves. Lying, on the other hand, can make us feel guilty or worried. Teaching children that **"being honest makes our hearts feel light and happy"** helps them understand that truthfulness brings peace of mind. Parents can reinforce this by saying, **"Honest people feel good because they know they did the right thing!"**

What Happens When We Lie?

Lying can cause problems, such as making others feel sad or leading to more lies. If a child tells a lie, they may have to tell more lies to cover it up. This can make them feel stressed. Teaching children that **"one small lie can grow into a big problem"** helps them understand why it's best to be honest from the start.

How to Be Honest in Everyday Life

Honesty isn't just about telling the truth—it's also about being fair and doing the right thing. If a child finds a toy that isn't theirs, they should return it instead of keeping it. If they make a mess, they should admit it and clean it up. Teaching preschoolers that **"honesty means making good choices even when no one is looking"** helps them develop strong character.

Learning to Admit Mistakes

Everyone makes mistakes, and that's okay! The important thing is to admit when we've done something wrong and try to fix it. If a child spills their juice, they should say, **"I spilled it. I'll help clean it up!"** instead of blaming someone else. Parents and teachers can remind children, **"It's okay to make mistakes, but it's important to be honest about them."**

Saying "I'm Sorry" When We Are Wrong

Honest people take responsibility for their actions. If a child hurts someone's feelings or breaks a rule, they should apologize and try to make things better. Teaching preschoolers that **"saying sorry shows honesty and kindness"** encourages them to take responsibility for their actions.

Telling the Truth Even When It's Hard

Sometimes, telling the truth can be difficult, especially if a child is afraid of getting in trouble. But being honest is always the right choice. Parents and teachers can create a safe space where children feel comfortable telling the truth by saying, **"I will always appreciate your honesty, even if you make a mistake."** This helps children feel secure in being truthful.

Rewarding Honesty with Praise

When children tell the truth, they should be praised for their honesty. Saying things like, **"Thank you for telling the truth! That was very brave of you,"** reinforces positive behavior. When children see that honesty is valued and appreciated, they are more likely to be truthful in the future.

Honesty Makes the World a Better Place

When everyone tells the truth, the world becomes a better and more trusting place. People feel safe, friendships grow stronger, and problems can be solved more easily. Teaching preschoolers that **"honesty is the key to trust and happiness"** helps them understand why being truthful is one of the most important values in life.

Section 13: Sharing and Being Kind to Others

1. What Is Sharing?

Sharing means giving a part of what we have to others so that everyone can enjoy it. It could be sharing toys with a friend, sharing crayons in class, or even sharing a snack with a sibling. When children learn to share, they become more caring and thoughtful individuals. Teaching preschoolers that **"sharing makes playtime more fun for everyone"** helps them understand why it's important.

Why Sharing Is Important

Sharing helps children make and keep friends. When we share, we show kindness, generosity, and respect for others. Imagine if a child has a box of crayons but doesn't share— other children might feel left out. Teaching kids that **"sharing makes others happy and helps us all have a good time"** encourages positive social behavior.

How Does Sharing Make Us Feel?

When we share, we feel good inside because we are doing something nice for someone else. Seeing a friend smile because we let them use our toy or gave them a turn makes us happy, too. Parents and teachers can remind children, **"Sharing fills our hearts with joy and makes the world a kinder place."**

Basic Concept of Respect in a Simple

Taking Turns is a Part of Sharing

Sometimes, we can't completely give something away, but we can take turns using it. If two children want to play with the same toy, they can learn to **"wait and share"** instead of arguing.

Teaching preschoolers to say, **"It's your turn now, and I'll have my turn next,"** helps them practice patience and fairness.

Being Kind Through Actions and Words

Kindness is not just about sharing things—it's also about using kind words and being gentle with others. Saying **"please"** and **"thank you,"** helping a friend who falls, or giving someone a compliment are all ways to be kind. Encouraging children to **"spread kindness like confetti"** makes them more mindful of their actions.

How Sharing Helps Us Build Friendships

Children who share are more likely to have strong friendships. When kids are willing to share their toys, games, and experiences, others enjoy being around them. Teaching preschoolers that **"friends love playing with kind sharers"** helps them understand that generosity makes friendships stronger.

Shine Your Light

What If We Don't Want to Share?

It's natural for children to feel attached to their belongings. Sometimes, they may not want to share, and that's okay. The key is teaching them to be fair—if a toy is very special, they can let others play with a different toy instead. Parents can say, **"It's okay to have special things, but let's find something else to share!"** to encourage balance.

Kindness in Different Situations

Kindness isn't just about sharing toys—it's also about helping others, using kind words, and showing respect. If a friend is sad, a child can cheer them up with a hug or kind words. If someone needs help carrying something, they can offer to help. Teaching children that **"kindness is like sunshine—it makes everything brighter"** helps them understand the power of small, kind acts.

How to Handle When Others Don't Share

Sometimes, other children might not want to share, and that can be frustrating. Instead of getting upset, preschoolers should learn to **ask politely, wait patiently, or play with something else**.

Teaching them to say, **"Can I have a turn after you?"** instead of grabbing teaches respect for others.

Sharing and Kindness Make the World Better

When we share and show kindness, we make our homes,

schools, and playgrounds happier places. Children who learn to share grow up to be caring, generous, and thoughtful adults. Reminding preschoolers that **"a little kindness goes a long way"** helps them develop a habit of being gracious and loving in all they do.

Section 14: Helping Others & Being a Good Friend

1. What Does It Mean to Help Others?

Helping others means doing something kind to make someone's day better. It can be as simple as picking up a friend's toy when it falls, allowing a younger sibling to put on their shoes, or holding the door open for someone. Teaching preschoolers that **"helping hands make the world a better place"** encourages them to be kind and helpful.

Why Is It Important to Help?

When we help others, we show that we care. Helping makes people feel happy and appreciated. If a friend is sad, giving them a hug or saying something nice can cheer them up. When children learn that **"a small act of kindness can make a big difference,"** they become more thoughtful and caring.

Being a Good Friend Means Helping

Good friends look out for each other. If a friend is struggling to put away their toys, helping them shows kindness. Sharing, taking turns, and saying nice things are all ways to be a good friend.

Parents and teachers can remind children, **"A good friend helps, shares, and cares."**

Basic Concept of Respect in a Simple

Helping at Home

Children can be great helpers at home! They can put their toys away, set the table for meals, or help feed a pet. When they help at home, they make life easier for their family. Saying, **"Helping at home shows love and responsibility,"** teaches preschoolers that their small efforts make a big impact.

Helping at School

In school, helping others makes the classroom a happy place. Children can help their teacher by cleaning up, passing out supplies, or being kind to classmates. If a friend forgets something, you can remind them. Encouraging children by saying, **"A helpful student is a great learner and friend!"** motivates them to be responsible.

Helping in the Community

Even young children can help in their community. They can pick up litter in the park, donate toys to kids in need, or say **"thank you"** to people who help them, like firefighters, doctors, and teachers. Teaching preschoolers that **"everyone can help make the world better"** inspires them to be kind citizens.

Listening & Understanding Others' Needs

Sometimes, people don't ask for help, but we can still notice when they need it. If a friend looks sad, asking, **"Are you okay?"** can make them feel better. If someone is struggling to carry something, offering to help is a great way to show kindness. Teaching children that **"good friends pay attention to others' feelings"** helps them become more caring.

Saying Kind Words to Help

Words can be powerful helpers, too! Saying **"Great job!"** or **"I believe in you!"** can encourage friends. Using kind words like **"please," "thank you,"** and **"I'm here for you"** makes people feel valued. Reminding preschoolers that **"words can help and heal"** teaches them that kindness isn't just in actions but also in what we say.

Helping Without Expecting a Reward

Helping others should come from the heart, not just because we want something in return. True kindness is helping because we want to, not because we expect praise or gifts. Parents and teachers can say, **"A real helper does good things just to make others happy!"** to encourage generosity.

Helping Others Makes the World a Better Place

When everyone helps each other, the world becomes a kinder and happier place. Teaching preschoolers that **"helping hands create happy hearts"** encourages them to spread kindness wherever they go. Whether at home, school, or in their community, small acts of kindness make a big difference.

Section 15: Using Polite Words & Good Manners

1. What Are Polite Words and Good Manners?

Polite words and good manners help people show kindness and respect to others. Saying things like **"please," "thank you,"** and **"excuse me"** makes people feel happy and appreciated. Good manners also include **being respectful, waiting for your turn, and speaking kindly to others.** Teaching preschoolers that **"politeness makes the world a friendlier place"** helps them understand why manners matter.

Why Are Good Manners Important?

Using good manners helps us get along with others. When we say **"thank you,"** it shows appreciation. When we say **"please,"** it makes requests sound kind instead of demanding. Good manners help us make friends, show respect, and create a positive environment at home and school. Reminding children that **"manners make people feel respected and happy"** encourages them to be polite.

Saying "Please" and "Thank You"

Saying **"please"** when asking for something makes it sound more respectful. For example, instead of saying, **"Give me the toy!"**, a child should say, **"Can I have the toy, please?"** Saying **"thank you"** shows appreciation when someone gives us something or helps us. Teaching preschoolers to use these words daily helps them develop a habit of politeness.

Saying "Excuse Me" and "Sorry"

"Excuse me" is a polite way to get someone's attention or to move past someone in a crowded space. Instead of pushing past a friend, a child should say, **"Excuse me, may I pass?"** Saying **"sorry"** when we make a mistake shows responsibility and care. Teaching children that **"apologizing makes things better"** helps them understand the importance of making amends.

Greeting Others Politely

Saying **"hello"** and **"goodbye"** in a friendly way makes people feel welcome. When children greet their teachers in the morning or say **"goodnight"** to their parents, it shows respect and warmth. Encouraging children to use greetings helps them practice social skills and build positive relationships.

Table Manners: Eating Politeness

Good manners also apply at mealtime. Using a napkin, chewing with the mouth closed, and saying **"may I have more, please?"** instead of grabbing food teaches respect at the table. Children should also wait for everyone to be served before eating. Teaching preschoolers that **"good table manners make mealtime enjoyable for everyone"** encourages them to be polite while eating.

Basic Concept of Respect in a Simple

Being a Good Listener

Listening when someone is talking is an important part of good manners. Interrupting is rude, but waiting for a turn to speak shows respect. Teaching children to look at the person speaking, nod, and wait patiently helps them become better communicators. Reminding preschoolers that **"listening is just as important as talking"** helps them understand the value of good communication.

Showing Respect for Others' Belongings

Being polite also means respecting what belongs to others. This includes asking before borrowing something, handling things gently, and returning items after use. If a child wants to use a friend's toy, they should say, **"May I play with this, please?"** instead of taking it without asking. Teaching preschoolers that **"respecting others' things shows kindness and responsibility"** helps them build positive relationships.

Saying "Kind Words" to Others

Kind words make people feel good. Saying **"You did a great job!"** or **"I like your drawing"** can brighten someone's day. Avoiding mean words, teasing, or yelling is also part of good manners. Teaching children that **"words can make people happy or sad, so choose them wisely"** helps them understand the power of their words.

Shine Your Light

Practicing Good Manners Every Day

The best way to learn good manners is by practicing them every day. Parents and teachers can encourage children by saying, **"Remember to use your magic words—please, thank you, excuse me, and sorry!"** The more children use polite words and good manners, the more natural it will feel. Teaching them that **"manners make the world kinder and more respectful"** helps them develop positive habits for life.

Section 16: Listening to Parents, Teachers, and Elders

1. What Does It Mean to Listen?

Listening means paying attention when someone is talking and trying to understand what they are saying. It's not just about hearing words—it's about focusing, thinking, and responding respectfully. When we listen, we show that we respect and care about the person speaking. Teaching preschoolers that **"good listening helps us learn and grow"** encourages them to be attentive.

Why Is Listening Important?

Listening helps us learn new things, stay safe, and build strong relationships. Parents, teachers, and elders share important lessons that help children understand the world. When we listen, we gain knowledge and wisdom. Teaching preschoolers that **"listening helps us make good choices"** encourages them to pay attention to what adults say.

How to Be a Good Listener

Being a good listener means looking at the speaker, staying quiet while they talk, and waiting for our turn to speak. It also means thinking about what is being said. Instead of interrupting, children can practice saying, **"I will wait my turn to talk"** to build patience and respect.

Shine Your Light

Listening to Parents at Home

Parents give important instructions to help children stay safe and grow up to be responsible. Listening to parents means following rules, like cleaning up toys, eating healthy food, and being kind to siblings. Teaching children that **"parents teach us because they love us"** helps them understand why listening to family is important.

Listening to Teachers at School

Teachers help children learn about numbers, letters, and the world around them. When students listen, they understand lessons better and do well in school. If a child talks while the teacher is speaking, they might miss something important. Reminding preschoolers that **"listening to the teacher helps us learn and have fun"** encourages good classroom behavior.

Listening to Elders in the Community

Grandparents, older relatives, and community elders have a lot of wisdom to share. They can tell interesting stories, teach life lessons, and give good advice. When children listen to elders, they learn important values like respect, kindness, and patience. Teaching preschoolers that **"elders have stories that help us learn about life"** helps them appreciate their wisdom.

What Happens When We Don't Listen?

When we don't listen, we might get into trouble or miss important information. Not listening to parents can lead to unsafe situations, like running into the street without looking. Not listening to teachers can make it harder to learn. Helping children understand that **"listening keeps us safe and helps us grow"** encourages them to be more attentive.

How to Show That We Are Listening

We can show we are listening by making eye contact, nodding, and answering politely. If a teacher gives instructions, repeating them back indicates understanding. If a grandparent shares a story, asking questions shows interest. Teaching preschoolers that **"good listeners make people feel important"** helps them develop strong communication skills.

Being Patient and Waiting to Speak

Sometimes, children want to talk while someone else is speaking. Teaching them to **wait their turn and not interrupt** is an important lesson in respect. A helpful phrase for kids is, **"I will listen first, then I can talk."** Practicing patience teaches children how to be respectful and considerate.

Listening Makes the World a Better Place

When we listen, we understand others better, avoid problems, and show respect. Good listeners make great friends, students, and family members. Teaching preschoolers that **"listening is a superpower that helps us learn, stay safe, and be kind"** encourages them to practice this important skill every day.

Section 17: Sharing and Taking Turns

1. What Does It Mean to Share?

Sharing means letting others use something that belongs to us. It could be a toy, a snack, or even a fun experience. When we share, we show kindness and make others feel happy. Teaching preschoolers that **"sharing makes playtime more fun for everyone"** helps them understand why sharing is important.

Why Is Sharing Important?

Sharing helps us make friends and build strong relationships. When we share, we learn to be kind, patient, and generous. It also helps everyone feel included. Teaching children that **"sharing shows we care about others"** encourages them to think about other people's feelings.

How to Share with Friends

When playing with toys, children can take turns using them instead of keeping them all to themselves. If a friend wants to play with a toy, they can say, **"You can play with it after me!"** instead of saying, **"No, it's mine!"** Learning to share helps children build friendships and enjoy playing together.

Taking Turns Makes Play Fair

Taking turns is another way to share. When playing on the

swings, waiting patiently instead of pushing ahead shows fairness. Saying, **"It's your turn now, and then it will be my turn,"** teaches preschoolers that everyone should have a chance to enjoy things.

How Sharing Feels for Others

When someone shares with us, it makes us feel happy and included. But when someone refuses to share, it can make others feel sad or left out. Teaching children that **"sharing makes everyone feel special"** helps them understand why being generous is important.

When It's Hard to Share

Sometimes, children find it difficult to share, especially if something is their favorite toy or snack. Parents and teachers can help by reminding them that **"sharing doesn't mean giving it away forever- it just means letting someone else enjoy it too."** Practicing sharing daily helps children get better at it.

Sharing at Home and School

Sharing isn't just for toys—it also means letting others have a turn speaking in a conversation, offering a sibling a piece of their snack, or letting a classmate borrow a crayon. Teaching preschoolers that **"sharing happens everywhere, not just on the playground"** helps them understand that kindness is a part of everyday life.

Using Kind Words When Sharing

Instead of grabbing or demanding, children should use kind words when asking to share. Saying, **"May I have a turn, please?"** or **"Would you like to play with me?"** helps them practice politeness. Teaching children that **"kind words make sharing easier"** encourages good communication.

How Sharing Helps Us Make Friends

Children who share are more likely to make and keep friends. When they share their toys, snacks, or play on the playground, other kids see them as kind and fun to be around. Reminding children that **"sharing brings friends together"** helps them see the positive side of being generous.

Sharing and Taking Turns Make the World a Better Place

When everyone shares, there are fewer arguments and more smiles. Whether at school, home, or in the community, sharing helps people feel connected and cared for. Teaching preschoolers that **"sharing is a superpower that spreads happiness"** encourages them to practice generosity every day.

Section 18: Being Kind and Helping Others

1. What Does It Mean to Be Kind?

Being kind means treating others with care, respect, and understanding. It includes saying nice things, helping when someone needs it, and showing love to family, friends, and even strangers. Teaching preschoolers that **"kindness makes the world a happier place"** helps them understand why it's important.

Why Is Kindness Important?

Kindness makes people feel good and helps build strong friendships. When we are kind, we make others happy, and in return, they are kind to us too. Teaching children that **"kindness spreads like sunshine"** encourages them to be caring in their daily lives.

Simple Ways to Show Kindness

Children can show kindness in many ways, such as sharing their toys, giving a hug to a friend, or saying **"thank you"** when someone helps them. Smiling, giving compliments, and using kind words also show kindness. Teaching preschoolers that **"small acts of kindness can make a big difference"** encourages them to be thoughtful.

Shine Your Light

Helping at Home

Being kind at home means helping parents, siblings, and even pets. Children can help by picking up their toys, setting the table, or comforting a sibling who is upset. When they help, they make the home a happier place. Teaching them that **"helping at home shows love and care"** encourages responsibility.

Helping at School

Kindness is important at school, too. Helping a friend who drops their crayons, waiting patiently in line, or sharing a book are ways to show kindness in the classroom. When children help their teacher by listening and following instructions, they create a positive learning environment.

Teaching preschoolers that **"helping at school makes learning fun for everyone"** encourages good behavior.

Being Kind to Friends

Friends are an important part of a child's life, and kindness helps friendships grow. If a friend feels sad, saying, **"Are you okay?"** or giving them a hug can make them feel better. Playing together, taking turns, and using kind words help children build strong friendships. Teaching preschoolers that **"a kind friend is a good friend"** encourages them to be compassionate.

Helping Those in Need

Some people need extra help, like elderly neighbors, younger siblings, or classmates who feel shy. Even small acts, like opening a door for someone or helping carry something, can make a big difference. Teaching children that **"helping others makes us feel good, too"** encourages a spirit of generosity.

The Magic of Saying Kind Words

Words have power, and saying things like **"I like your drawing!"** or **"You did a great job!"** can brighten someone's day. Avoiding mean words and choosing kind ones helps everyone feel happy. Teaching preschoolers that **"kind words are like hugs for the heart"** reminds them to speak kindly.

Kindness Can Change the World

One act of kindness can inspire another. When a child helps a friend, that friend may help someone else, creating a chain of kindness. Teaching children that **"kindness is a gift we can give every day"** encourages them to make the world a better place.

Practicing Kindness Every Day

The best way to be kind is to practice it daily. Parents and teachers can remind children to **"be kind, be helpful, and spread joy!"** The more children practice kindness, the more natural it becomes. Teaching preschoolers that **"kindness is like a superpower—it makes everyone happy"** helps them develop a lifelong habit of helping others.

Section 19: Saying "Please," "Thank You," and "Excuse Me"

1. Why Are Polite Words Important?

Polite words help us show respect and kindness to others. They make conversations pleasant and help people feel appreciated. When children learn to say **"please," "thank you,"** and **"excuse me,"** they build good manners that will help them in school, at home, and in the community.

Teaching preschoolers that **"polite words make people happy"** encourages them to use them often.

The Magic of Saying "Please"

Saying **"please"** is a way to ask for something nicely and respectfully. Instead of demanding, **"Give me that!"**, saying, **"Can I have that, please?"** sounds much kinder. When we use **"please,"** people are more likely to help us or share with us. Teaching children that **"saying 'please' makes others want to help"** encourages them to use this word daily.

Why Saying "Thank You" Matters

When someone does something nice for us, giving them a **"thank you"** shows appreciation. Whether a friend shares a toy or a parent makes dinner, saying **"thank you"** helps people feel valued. Teaching children that **"thank you is a way to show we are grateful** helps them understand the

Basic Concept of Respect in a Simple

importance of appreciation.

Using "Excuse Me" in Conversations

Sometimes, we need to get someone's attention, but we don't want to be rude. Saying **"excuse me"** before speaking helps us be polite. For example, instead of interrupting a conversation, a child can say, **"Excuse me, may I talk now?"** Teaching preschoolers that **"excuse me shows respect when we need to speak** helps them learn patience and good manners.

"Excuse Me" When Moving Around Others

When we walk past someone or accidentally bump into them, saying **"excuse me"** is a polite way to acknowledge them. It shows that we care about being respectful. Teaching children that **"excuse me helps us be kind in busy places,** encourages them to be mindful of others.

Practicing Good Manners at Home

Home is the first place where children learn good manners. Parents can encourage children to say **"please"** when asking for food, **"thank you"** when receiving help, and **"excuse me"** when they need to interrupt. Teaching preschoolers that **"manners start at home"** helps them develop

polite habits.

Shine Your Light

Using Polite Words at School

At school, polite words help children get along with teachers and classmates. Saying **"please"** when borrowing a crayon, **"thank you"** when receiving help, and **"excuse me"** when needing to pass by a friend are all important habits. Teaching children that **"good manners make school a happy place"** encourages them to be respectful learners.

How Politeness Helps Make Friends

People like to be around those who are polite and kind. Saying **"please"** when asking to play, **"thank you"** when someone shares, and **"excuse me"** when needing to talk helps children build friendships. Teaching preschoolers that **"politeness helps us make and keep friends"**

encourages them to use kind words with others.

Good Manners in Public Places

Whether at a store, park, or restaurant, using polite words shows respect for everyone around us. Saying **"excuse me"** when walking past someone, **"please"** when ordering food, and **"thank you"** when someone holds a door open are small acts that make a big difference. Teaching preschoolers that **"politeness makes the world a nicer place"** helps them understand the power of good manners.

Making Politeness a Daily Habit

The more we use polite words, the easier it becomes. Parents

Basic Concept of Respect in a Simple

and teachers can remind children to practice saying **"please," "thank you," and "excuse me"** in everyday conversations. Teaching preschoolers that **"good manners are like magic words that bring kindness everywhere"** encourages them to make politeness a lifelong habit.

Section 20 A Thankful Heart is a Happy Heart – Teaching Gratitude and Appreciation

Gratitude is one of the most important values we can teach children, as it helps them develop a positive mindset and appreciate the world around them. A child who learns to be thankful grows up to be more content, kind, and compassionate. When children recognize the good things in their lives—whether big or small—they develop a sense of happiness that stays with them.

Gratitude isn't just about saying "thank you"; it's about feeling and showing appreciation in daily life.

One of the first steps in teaching gratitude is helping children notice the blessings they already have. Many young kids naturally focus on what they **want** rather than what they **have**. Parents and teachers can guide them by encouraging them to reflect on simple joys, such as a warm meal, a hug from a loved one, or the laughter of a friend. Teaching children to recognize these little moments helps them realize that happiness isn't found in material things but in appreciating what they already have.

Saying "thank you" is an easy way to express gratitude, and it's an important habit for children to develop. By encouraging kids to thank their parents, teachers, and friends, they learn to acknowledge the kindness of others. This not only strengthens relationships but also makes them more aware of the love and care they receive daily. Expressing thanks makes both the giver and receiver feel happy, creating a cycle of kindness and appreciation.

Gratitude also teaches children to be more empathetic. When

they understand how much effort someone puts into helping them, whether it's a teacher preparing lessons or a parent cooking dinner, they begin to appreciate the value of kindness. This understanding fosters respect for others and encourages them to return kindness with kindness. A grateful heart naturally leads to generosity, as children who appreciate what they have are more likely to share with others.

Another essential lesson is finding gratitude even in difficult situations. Life isn't always easy, and there will be moments when children feel disappointed, sad, or frustrated. However, teaching them to look for silver linings—like learning something new from a challenge or having supportive friends and family—helps them develop resilience. Gratitude shifts focus from **what's missing** to **what's present**, making even tough times a little brighter.

A wonderful way to nurture gratitude in children is by making it a daily practice. Parents and teachers can encourage kids to keep a **gratitude journal**, where they write or draw things they are thankful for each day. Another fun activity is a **gratitude jar**, where children can drop notes about things that made them happy. These small practices help children develop the habit of focusing on the positive aspects of life.

Acts of kindness also go hand in hand with gratitude. When children learn to help others—whether by sharing toys, helping a friend, or making a thank-you card—they experience the joy of giving. Gratitude isn't just about receiving; it's also about showing appreciation through actions. Teaching children that their kindness can make someone's day better reinforces the idea that gratitude creates happiness for both the giver and the receiver.

Shine Your Light

Nature is another wonderful teacher of gratitude. Encouraging children to appreciate the beauty of a sunset, the sound of birds chirping, or the shade of a tree helps them see that there is so much to be thankful for. Taking a simple "gratitude walk" and noticing the wonders around them instills a deeper appreciation for the world. Learning to say **"thank you" to nature** by caring for plants, picking up litter, or feeding birds can also strengthen their connection to the environment.

The more children practice gratitude, the more naturally it becomes a part of their mindset. Over time, they begin to see the world through a lens of appreciation, noticing goodness even in ordinary moments. A thankful heart leads to a more positive attitude, stronger relationships, and a deeper sense of joy. When children understand that true happiness comes from within, rather than from material things, they develop a lasting sense of contentment.

Ultimately, gratitude is a lifelong gift. A child who learns to be thankful grows into an adult who values kindness, cherishes relationships, and finds joy in everyday life. By teaching children that **a thankful heart is a happy heart**, we help them build a foundation for a life filled with appreciation, positivity, and genuine happiness.

"What is Respect? – Teaching the Basic Concept of Respect in a Simple Way"

1. Respect is treating others the way you would like to be treated—with kindness, care, and understanding. It means recognizing that everyone has value, feelings, and a right to be heard. When you respect someone, you listen to them, speak kindly, and consider their thoughts and feelings. Respect builds trust, strengthens relationships, and helps people feel safe and appreciated.

2. At its heart, respect starts with awareness. When you become aware that other people have their own experiences, hopes, and struggles, just like you, it becomes easier to treat them with care. It's like holding a mirror up to yourself and realizing that others deserve the same treatment you wish for: honesty, fairness, and kindness.

3. Respect doesn't mean you have to agree with everyone. It simply means you allow space for differences. For example, if someone believes something different from what you do, respect means listening without mocking or arguing. You can disagree respectfully by being calm, curious, and open-minded.

4. One of the easiest ways to show respect is through your tone of voice and body language. Looking someone in the eye, speaking clearly, not interrupting, and using polite words like "please," "thank you," and "excuse me" all send a message of care and dignity. These small actions say, "I see you. You matter."

5. Respect isn't only about how we treat others—it also

includes how we treat ourselves.

Self-respect means knowing your own worth and making choices that protect your body, mind, and spirit. When you respect yourself, you avoid harmful behavior and surround yourself with people who uplift you. Respecting others begins with respecting yourself.

6. You can show respect to adults, like parents, teachers, and elders, by listening when they speak, following rules, and responding politely even when you're upset. These adults have life experience and often care deeply about your growth. Respecting them creates a sense of harmony and invites guidance that can help you thrive.

7. Respect is also shown by honoring people's boundaries. This means giving space when someone needs it, not pressuring them to do something they're uncomfortable with, and asking for permission before borrowing or touching something that isn't yours. It shows maturity and builds trust.

8. In your community, respect means taking care of shared spaces, helping those in need, and treating everyone with fairness regardless of their background, beliefs, or abilities. Simple acts like holding the door open, cleaning up after yourself, or greeting your neighbors kindly create a culture of respect that uplifts everyone.

9. When respect becomes a habit, life becomes smoother and more joyful. Fewer arguments happen, more people feel safe around you, and you begin to develop stronger friendships and family bonds. People notice when you are respectful, and they are more likely to treat you the same way in return.

10. So, what is respect? It's a powerful, everyday way to show love and honor to others, to the world, and to yourself. When you practice it regularly, you build a foundation of character that supports success in school, family, friendships, and even your future career. A respectful heart is a wise and peaceful heart.

Basic Concept of Respect in a simple Way

Educational Guide for Teenagers: Respect, Understanding, and Supporting Elders, Teachers, and Parents for Your Highest Potential

Teenagers, with practical activities and reflections included to deepen understanding and foster respect:

1. Respect for teachers, parents, and elders is fundamental because they are the guiding stars in our lives. They carry wisdom from their experiences and serve as mentors on our journey. Showing respect through kind words, listening attentively, and expressing gratitude - builds trust and opens the door to learning. Take a moment each day to thank the elders around you, whether verbally or through a simple gesture, acknowledging their role in your growth. Remember, respect is the first step toward building meaningful relationships and understanding their deeper spiritual purpose.

Respect for teachers, parents, and elders is the cornerstone of a harmonious and meaningful life. These individuals are like guiding stars, illuminating our path with their wisdom and life experiences. They serve as mentors who help us navigate the challenges of growth and learning, offering support and guidance rooted in love and understanding. Showing respect whether through kind words, attentive listening, or simple acts of gratitude - strengthens our bonds and fosters trust. When we acknowledge their contributions with heartfelt appreciation, we not only honor their efforts but also open our hearts to deeper understanding and connection. Respect is more than politeness; it is a recognition of their spiritual role as guides and guardians of wisdom. By cultivating this respect daily, we nurture relationships that are grounded in love, gratitude, and mutual growth, ultimately recognizing the divine spark within each person and appreciating the sacred purpose they serve in our lives.

2. Recognize that teachers, parents, and elders are not just authority figures but are also spiritual beings who have faced their own struggles and triumphs. They carry inner strength, love, and lessons that can inspire your growth. To deepen this understanding, try reflecting on their life stories or asking them about their journeys. This helps you see beyond external behaviors and develop compassion. For example, ask yourself: *What can I learn from their experiences?* Appreciating their spiritual wisdom helps us foster patience and gratitude, essential qualities for your personal development.

It's important to recognize that teachers, parents, and elders are more than just authority figures; they are also spiritual beings who have navigated their own paths filled with both struggles and triumphs. Behind their words and actions lie stories of resilience, love, and wisdom that can profoundly inspire our growth. By taking a moment to reflect on their life journeys or asking them about their experiences, we begin to see beyond their external roles and realize the depth of their inner strength. This understanding fosters compassion, patience, and gratitude - qualities that are essential for our personal development. Asking ourselves,

"What can I learn from their experiences?" opens our hearts to their wisdom and reminds us that everyone is on a unique journey. Appreciating the spiritual depth of those who guide us helps us grow in humility and love, enriching our lives and strengthening our connection with others.

3. Teachers and parents can support you best by approaching you with empathy and open communication. If you're facing challenges or uncertainties, share your feelings honestly. They can help guide you mentally by teaching you to think positively, manage stress, and believe in your own potential. Physically, they can help you develop healthy habits- like balanced eating, regular exercise, and enough sleep-that boost your energy and mental clarity. Remember, their goal is to nurture your highest aspirations while respecting your unique spiritual path. Practice asking questions and expressing your needs-they are there to help you succeed.

That's a strong and meaningful foundation for your **Educational Guide for Teenagers**. Here's a continuation and expansion on your third point, keeping the same warm tone and deep purpose while also integrating **practical activities and reflection prompts** for teens to foster **respect, understanding, and support** for elders, teachers, and parents.

How Elders, Teachers, and Parents Support Your Highest Self

Teachers and parents play a vital role in nurturing both your personal and spiritual development. Their guidance goes beyond rules and homework-they are here to support your mental, emotional, and physical well-being. When you face challenges like self-doubt, anxiety, or confusion, they can offer wisdom and tools to help you grow. The key is open communication. Being honest about your struggles and questions helps them understand how to best support you.

Mentally, they help you shift negative thinking into possibility thinking. They remind you of your strengths and potential when you forget. They might teach you how to focus better, how to set goals, or how to respond to stress with calmness. Emotionally, they offer stability and encouragement when things feel overwhelming. Even when they correct you, it usually comes from a place of care and protection.

Physically, your parents and teachers care about your lifestyle because it affects how you learn, feel, and function. Good sleep, nutritious food, daily movement, and less screen time may seem small-but they create the foundation for a strong mind and body. Elders may encourage you to take breaks, go outside, or even teach you calming practices like stretching, prayer, or breathing techniques they've used for decades.

Spiritually, they may guide you with values that build integrity, patience, self-discipline, and compassion. Even if you don't share the same beliefs, their wisdom can help you shape your own values. Listening deeply to the way they live and speak gives insight into how to live meaningfully and consciously. They want you to become your best self, not a copy of them, but the most awakened version of *you*.

But they can't help if you don't let them in. Practice sharing your feelings instead of bottling them up. Say things like, "I've been feeling overwhelmed lately. Can I talk to you about it?" or "I'm struggling to stay motivated. Do you have any advice?" When you communicate with sincerity, you invite a more compassionate and helpful response.

Equally important is learning how to **ask questions with curiosity**, not criticism. Instead of "Why are you always on my case?" ask, "Can you help me understand why this is important to you?" That shift in tone shows maturity and opens space for mutual respect. It transforms conversations from conflict into connection.

Remember, they are not perfect. Your teachers and parents are also learning-sometimes still healing their own childhoods or balancing many responsibilities. When you view them as human, with their own needs and hopes, it deepens your empathy. You might be surprised how much closer you feel once you see them not just as adults but as people.

Reflection Prompt:

- What is one challenge I'm currently facing that I haven't shared with a trusted adult?

- How could I express my feelings in a respectful, open-hearted way?

Basic Concept of Respect in a Simple

Practical Activities:

1. Weekly Check-In Journal:

 Each Sunday, write down one thing you're grateful for from a parent, teacher, or elder. Reflect on how they supported you that week. This helps build awareness of the support you receive, even if it's subtle.

2. Conversation Starter Cards:

Create 3–5 index cards with questions like:

- "What was life like when you were my age?"

- "What's one lesson you learned the hard way?"

  Use these to start meaningful conversations with elders and teachers.

3. "Healthy Me" Checklist:

With a parent or teacher, make a simple weekly tracker:

- Hours of sleep

- Daily movement

- Water intake

- Moments of quiet reflection

  Review it together to see where small improvements can help your focus and well-being.

"What is Respect? – Teaching the Basic Concept of Respect in a Simple Way"

This version is ideal for teens or adaptable for younger audiences, too.

1. Respect is treating others the way you would like to be treated, with kindness, care, and understanding. It means recognizing that everyone has value, feelings, and a right to be heard. When you respect someone, you listen to them, speak kindly, and consider their thoughts and feelings. Respect builds trust, strengthens relationships, and helps people feel safe and appreciated.

2. At its heart, respect starts with awareness. When you become aware that other people have their own experiences, hopes, and struggles, just like you, it becomes easier to treat them with care. It's like holding a mirror up to yourself and realizing that others deserve the same treatment you wish for: honesty, fairness, and kindness.

3. Respect doesn't mean you have to agree with everyone. It simply means you allow space for differences. For example, if someone believes something different than you do, respect means listening without mocking or arguing. You can disagree respectfully by being calm, curious, and open-minded.

4. One of the easiest ways to show respect is through your tone of voice and body language. Looking someone in the eye, speaking clearly, not interrupting, and using polite words like "please," "thank you," and "excuse me" all send a message of care and dignity. These small actions say, "I see you. You matter."

5. Respect isn't only about how we treat others. It also includes how we treat ourselves. Self-respect means knowing your own worth and making choices that protect your body, mind, and spirit. When you respect yourself, you avoid harmful behavior and surround yourself with people who uplift you. Respecting others begins with respecting yourself.

 6. You can show respect to adults, like parents, teachers, and elders, by listening when they speak, following rules, and responding politely even when you're upset. These adults have life experience and often care deeply about your growth. Respecting them creates a sense of harmony and invites guidance that can help you thrive.

7. Respect is also shown by honoring people's boundaries. This means giving space when someone needs it, not pressuring them to do something they're uncomfortable with, and asking for permission before borrowing or touching something that isn't yours. It shows maturity and builds trust.

 8. In your community, respect means taking care of shared spaces, helping those in need, and treating everyone with fairness regardless of their background, beliefs, or abilities. Simple acts like holding the door open, cleaning up after yourself, or greeting your neighbors kindly create a culture of respect that uplifts everyone.

 9. When respect becomes a habit, life becomes smoother and more joyful. Fewer arguments happen, more people feel safe around you, and you begin to develop stronger friendships and family bonds. People notice when you are respectful—and they are more likely to treat you the same way in return.

10. So, what is respect? It's a powerful, everyday way to show love and honor—to others, to the world, and to yourself. When you practice it regularly, you build a foundation of character that supports success in school, family, friendships, and even your future career. A respectful heart is a wise and peaceful heart.

Pointers on Visuals:

Respectful Interaction Illustration:

An image of a young person respectfully listening to an elder or teacher, showing gratitude and humility through body language and facial expressions.

Door Opening Symbol:

A visual of a door opening to a bright, warm light symbolizes the unlocking of wisdom and the journey toward one's highest self.

Tree of Growth:

A tree with roots labeled "Respect," "Humility," "Gratitude," and branches representing growth into wisdom, calmness, and power.

Heart and Hand Symbols:

A heart with hands reaching out to elders and teachers, symbolizing sharing love, kindness, and mutual respect.

Basic Concept of Respect in a Simple

Community of People:

A diverse group of people supporting each other, symbolizing collective growth and creating a compassionate world.

Hooks (Captivating Openers):

"What if the key to becoming your best self is simply respecting and learning from those who came before you?

"Discover how small acts of gratitude and humility can unlock your greatest potential!"

"The secret to a brighter world starts with respect and understanding. Are you ready to open the door?"

"Imagine a world where everyone supports each other—building strength through kindness and respect."

"Your journey to greatness begins with a simple act: honoring others with respect and love."** Absolutely! Here are short motivational quotes, storytelling ideas, and interactive activities to reinforce the message about respect, understanding, and growth:

Short Motivational Quotes

"Respect opens the door to wisdom and love." "Supporting others helps us grow into our best selves."

"A humble heart and grateful spirit build powerful character." "When we honor our elders, we honor our future." "Kindness and respect are the keys to a brighter world." "Greatness begins with gratitude and humility."

Shine Your Light

"Supporting others is the path to true strength."

"Every act of respect plants a seed for a better tomorrow." "Wisdom is a gift we receive when we listen with an open heart." "Together, respect and love create a world worth living in."

Storytelling Ideas

1. The Key to the Kingdom

Tell a story about a young person who finds a mysterious door that symbolizes their highest self. The key? Respect, humility, and gratitude. When they unlock the door, they discover wisdom, peace, and power inside.

2. The Tree of Growth

Create a story about a young sapling growing into a mighty tree with roots named respect, humility, and kindness. The tree's strength and beauty come from nurturing these roots daily through acts of love and understanding.

3. The Gift of Wisdom

Share a story of an elder who shares a life lesson with a young person. The young person learns that by listening and showing gratitude, they gain wisdom that helps them become calm, wise, and strong.

4. The Circle of Support

Narrate a story of a community coming together, supporting each other with respect and kindness, creating a brighter, more compassionate world for everyone.

Basic Concept of Respect in a Simple

Interactive Activities

1. Respect Role-Play

Children act out scenarios where they show respect, gratitude, and humility toward elders or teachers. Afterward, discuss how it felt and what they learned.

2. Gratitude Circle

Form a circle where each person shares something they're grateful for about someone else in the group, fostering appreciation and mutual respect.

3. Kindness Challenge

Encourage children to perform small acts of kindness and gratitude daily—writing notes, helping a peer, or thanking someone—and share their experiences.

4. "Respect the Elder" Poster

Create a poster or mural where children draw or write ways they can show respect and kindness to elders and teachers. Display it prominently.

5. Story Sharing

Invite children to share stories or memories of someone they respect and admire. Discuss how those acts of respect and understanding made a difference.

Key messages and the importance of empathy and open communication between parents, teachers, and teenagers:

Shine Your Light

This paragraph emphasizes that teachers and parents can be most effective in supporting teenagers when they approach them with empathy and a willingness to listen openly. When young people are facing challenges or feeling uncertain, it's important for them to feel safe sharing their emotions honestly, knowing they will be met with understanding rather than judgment. Supportive adults can guide teenagers both mentally and physically—mentally by encouraging positive thinking, stress management, and self-belief; physically, by promoting healthy habits like balanced nutrition, regular exercise, and sufficient sleep. The core message is that their role is to nurture the teen's highest potential and respect their individual spiritual journey. Encouraging teenagers to ask questions and communicate their needs helps build trust and teaches them to take ownership of their growth. Ultimately, supportive adults are there to empower young people to succeed, flourish, and realize their unique purpose in life.

4. To reach your highest potential, it's essential to create a supportive environment. Teachers and parents can encourage your talents and passions, helping you set goals aligned with your purpose. Develop routines that strengthen your mind and body: meditate daily for clarity, journal your thoughts, or practice mindfulness. Physically, stay active and nourish your body with healthy foods—these habits build resilience and confidence. Reflect regularly: *What do I truly love? What are my goals?* When guided with love and encouragement, you'll find yourself growing into a wise, compassionate person ready to face life's challenges.

Certainly! Here are pointers on what visuals and hooks you can use to make this message engaging and impactful, along with a brief explanation of the content:

Basic Concept of Respect in a Simple

Pointers on Visuals:

Illustrations of a Supportive Conversation:

A teacher and student sharing a heart-to-heart, with speech bubbles showing words like "I'm here to help" or "Tell me how you feel."

Healthy Habits Icon Set:

Icons representing balanced meals, exercise, sleep, and stress management—showing the physical support side.

Pathway or Ladder Visual:

A pathway or ladder symbolizes growth, with milestones labeled "Positive Thinking," "Self-Belief," and "Healthy Habits," representing how support guides progress.

Question and Expression Symbols:

Speech bubbles or question marks encourage asking questions with an open hand or listening ear icon, emphasizing open communication.

Empathy and Connection Illustration:

A caring adult listens attentively to a teenager, showing empathy and understanding.

Hooks (Captivating Openers):

"Did you know? The way adults support you can make all the difference in your growth!" "Imagine having someone who truly listens and helps you unlock your full potential—that's what support looks like!"

"What if the biggest help you could get is just an honest conversation?"

"Supporting your dreams starts with understanding and caring. Here's how parents and teachers can do that for you."

"Feeling uncertain? Here's how caring adults are ready to guide you every step of the way."

Brief Explanation of the Paragraph:

This paragraph highlights how teachers and parents can best support teenagers by approaching them with kindness, empathy, and open communication. When teens face challenges or uncertainties, sharing their feelings honestly allows adults to guide them mentally, teaching positive thinking and stress management and boosting confidence. Physically, adults help develop healthy habits like nutritious eating, exercise, and sleep, which improve energy and clarity. The main goal is to nurture each teen's highest potential while respecting their individual spiritual and personal journey. Encouraging teenagers to ask questions and express their needs creates a supportive environment where they feel empowered to succeed and grow into their best selves.

5. Respect and understanding are keys to unlocking your highest self. When you honor the elders and teachers in your life, you open the door to their wisdom and love. Approach them with humility and gratitude, and you'll discover lessons that shape your character, lessons that help you become calm, wise, and powerful. Remember, your journey is also about supporting others: listen to their stories, show kindness, and share your gratitude. Together, with mutual respect and love, we can grow into the best versions of ourselves and create a brighter, more compassionate world.

Certainly! Here are pointers on visuals and hooks to make this message engaging and memorable, along with some ideas to capture attention effectively:

Pointers on Visuals:

Respectful Interaction Illustration:

An image of a young person respectfully listening to an elder or teacher, showing gratitude and humility through body language and facial expressions.

Door Opening Symbol:

A visual of a door opening to a bright, warm light symbolizes the unlocking of wisdom and the journey toward one's highest self.

Tree of Growth:

A tree with roots labeled "Respect," "Humility," "Gratitude," and branches representing growth into wisdom, calmness, and power.

Heart and Hand Symbols:

A heart with hands reaching out to elders and teachers, symbolizing sharing love, kindness, and mutual respect.

Community of People:

A diverse group of people supporting each other, symbolizing collective growth and creating a compassionate world.

Hooks (Captivating Openers):

"What if the key to becoming your best self is simply respecting and learning from those who came before you?

"Discover how small acts of gratitude and humility can unlock your greatest potential!

"The secret to a brighter world starts with respect and understanding. Are you ready to open the door?"

"Imagine a world where everyone supports each other, building strength through kindness and respect."

"Your journey to greatness begins with a simple act: honoring others with respect and love."

Here's a set of practical activities, reflections, and a mantra designed for teenagers to reinforce respect, understanding, and support for elders, teachers, and parents on their journey toward their highest potential:

Practical Activities and Daily Reflections

1. Gratitude Reflection:

Each morning or evening, write down three things you appreciate about your parents, teachers, or elders. Reflect on their efforts, wisdom, or kindness. This simple practice helps cultivate respect and gratitude, strengthening your connection with them.

2. Listening Exercise:

Choose someone you look up to, your parent, teacher, or elder, and spend 10 minutes actively listening to their stories or advice without interrupting. Focus on understanding their experiences and feelings. Afterward, thank them genuinely and share what you learned.

3. Acts of Kindness:

Make it a goal to do one act of kindness each day for someone older, help with chores, write a thank-you note, or give a compliment. Small acts build respect and deepen your appreciation for their role in your life.

4. Meditation or Mindfulness:

Spend 5-10 minutes daily practicing breathing exercises or mindfulness. Focus on sending loving energy to your elders and teachers, visualizing your gratitude and respect flowing toward them. This helps cultivate compassion and patience.

5. Goal-Setting Journal:

Write down your personal goals and identify how your elders and teachers can support you. Reflect on what guidance or encouragement you need from them, and think of ways to communicate your needs respectfully. This prepares you for meaningful conversations about your growth.

Daily Reflection Questions

What have I learned from my elders and teachers today? How can I show more respect and appreciation for them?

What qualities do I admire in my elders, and how can I develop those myself? In what ways can I support and uplift others around me?

How can I honor my own unique spiritual journey while respecting others?

Mantra for Respect and Growth

"With an open heart, I honor the wisdom of those who guide me. I am grateful for their love, strength, and lessons. I embrace my journey of growth and support others on theirs. Together, we rise in compassion, respect, and divine purpose."

You're right! Including parents explicitly is essential. Here's a revised version of the practical activities, reflections, and mantra, now emphasizing respect and understanding for parents along with elders and teachers:

Practical Activities and Daily Reflections for Respecting Parents, Elders, and Teachers

1. Gratitude Reflection:

Each day, write down three specific things you appreciate about your parents, whether it's their love, patience, guidance, or sacrifices. Take a moment to truly feel gratitude for everything they do to support your growth. This habit nurtures respect and deepens your connection with them.

2. Listening Exercise:

Spend 10 minutes actively listening to your parents or elders, asking about their life stories, lessons, or advice. Focus on understanding their experiences and feelings without interruptions. Afterward, thank them sincerely, showing appreciation for their wisdom and care.

3. Acts of Kindness:

Perform one act of kindness each day for your parents or elders, help with chores, write a heartfelt note, or simply spend quality time with them. Small gestures of love and respect build stronger bonds and show your appreciation.

4. Mindful Connection:

Practice 5-10 minutes of mindfulness or meditation daily, sending loving energy to your parents and elders. Visualize gratitude and respect flowing from your heart to theirs, strengthening your emotional bond and cultivating patience.

5. Goal-Setting for Growth:

Write down your personal goals and identify how your parents and teachers can support your highest aspirations. Think of respectful ways to communicate your needs and aspirations to them, fostering mutual understanding and encouragement.

Daily Reflection Questions

What have I learned from my parents today?

Shine Your Light

How can I show my appreciation and respect for my parents and elders?

What qualities in my parents do I admire, and how can I embody those qualities? In what ways can I support and uplift my family today?

How can I honor my own spiritual journey while respecting my parents' guidance?

Mantra for Respect and Highest Potential

"With love and gratitude, I honor my parents, elders, and teachers. I see their divine essence and appreciate their sacrifices. I am grateful for their wisdom and support. Together, we grow in compassion, respect, and divine purpose, creating a harmonious world of understanding and love."

Great questions! Supporting teenagers through their challenges while maintaining respect, trust, and healthy boundaries can be complex, especially in today's technology-driven world. Here are some thoughtful approaches for parents to help teenagers with their problems, approach them when they're wrong, and foster trust and guidance:

1. Create a Safe and Open Environment

Teenagers often feel misunderstood or judged, especially when they face problems. As a parent, foster a space where they feel safe to share their feelings without fear of harsh judgment or punishment. Show genuine interest in their world-listen more than you speak, and avoid interrupting or dismissing their feelings. When they sense your unconditional support, they'll be more likely to come to you when they need help.

2. Approach with Empathy and Respect

When addressing issues or mistakes, approach your teen with empathy. Instead of immediately pointing out what they did wrong, ask questions like, "Can you help me understand what was going on?" or "How are you feeling about this?" This helps them feel respected and understood. Remember, teenagers are developing their own sense of independence, so respect their feelings even if you disagree.

3. Use Disciplinary Actions as Guidance, Not Punishment

Discipline should be about guiding and teaching, not punishment. When your teen makes a mistake, explain why their actions may be harmful or inappropriate, then discuss healthier choices. For example, if they overuse technology, instead of cutting it off abruptly, talk about balance and set clear, reasonable boundaries together. Involving them in setting rules helps them feel respected and more willing to cooperate.

4. Address Overuse of Technology with Education and Boundaries

Technology is a powerful tool but can be overwhelming. Instead of banning it outright, educate them about healthy habits. Encourage activities like outdoor play, reading, or creative pursuits. Set agreed-upon limits to no devices during family meals or an hour before bed—and explain why these boundaries promote better focus, sleep, and mental health. Show understanding of their need for connection, but also emphasize the importance of balance.

5. Build Trust by Leading with Example and Patience

Trust is built when parents demonstrate integrity, patience, and consistency. Show your teen that you also seek advice, learn from mistakes, and respect others' perspectives. Share your own challenges and how you handle them. When they see you practicing humility and openness, they'll be more likely to trust your guidance and seek your advice. Remember, trust takes time, patience, and consistency.

6. Encourage Critical Thinking and Self-Reflection

Help your teen develop their own judgment by asking guiding questions rather than giving direct solutions. For example, "What do you think is the best way to handle this?" or "What do you feel you could do differently next time?" This empowers them to develop their problem-solving skills and trust their own judgment, knowing you support their growth.

7. Respect Their Need for Independence While Offering Guidance

Teenagers are eager to establish independence but still need guidance. Respect their desire to handle things on their own, but remind them that they can always come to you for support. Use phrases like, "I trust you to make your own decisions, but I'm here if you need advice or support." This reassures them that they are trusted and loved, which encourages open communication.

Basic Concept of Respect in a Simple

Summary for Parents:

Create a safe, non-judgmental space for open dialogue. Approach mistakes with empathy and respect.

Set boundaries about technology, explaining its importance. Model humility and patience to build trust.

Encourage independent thinking through guiding questions.

Offer support without overstepping, respecting their growing independence.

Here are conversation starters and guidelines for respectful discipline that parents can use to approach teenagers effectively, especially when discussing sensitive issues like technology overuse, mistakes, or independence:

Conversation Starters for Difficult Topics

1. Addressing Overuse of Technology:

"I've noticed you spend a lot of time on your devices lately. Can we talk about how you're feeling and ways we can find a balance that works for both of us?"

"What do you enjoy most about your screen time? How do you think it affects your mood or focus?"

"Would you be open to trying some activities together that don't involve screens? I'd love to spend quality time with you."

2. Discussing Mistakes or Bad Decisions:

"Everyone makes mistakes. Can you tell me what happened from your perspective?" "How are you feeling about this? What do you think you could do differently next time?"

"I'm here to help you figure out what to do next. Let's work together to find a good solution."

3. Building Trust and Independence:

"I trust you to make your own choices, but I also want you to know I'm here if you need advice or support."

"What's something you're proud of today? Is there anything you want to talk about or need help with?"

"How do you see your goals? How can I support you in reaching them?"

4. Explaining Boundaries and Rules:

"Can we talk about why I set certain boundaries around technology? I want to make sure you understand it's for your well-being."

"What do you think about the rules we have? Do you feel they're fair, or do you have suggestions?"

"Let's find a way to make these boundaries work for both of us so you feel respected and supported."

Basic Concept of Respect in a Simple

Guidelines for Respectful Discipline

Use "I" Statements:

Instead of accusing or blaming, express how you feel and what you observe.

"I feel worried when I see you on your phone late at night because I care about your sleep and health."

Focus on Behavior, Not Character:

Address specific actions rather than labeling the teenager.

"Leaving your clothes on the floor makes it hard for everyone to keep the room tidy," instead of "You're always messy."

Offer Choices and Involve Them:

Give your teen options to foster independence.

"Would you prefer to do your homework now or after dinner? Let's pick a time that works for you."

Explain the Why:

Help them understand the reasons behind rules or boundaries.

"We limit screen time because too much can affect your focus and sleep. I want you to be healthy and energized."

Stay Calm and Patient:

Approach discipline with patience, avoiding anger or frustration.

"I understand you're upset, but let's take a few minutes to calm down and talk about this calmly."

Encourage Reflection:

Ask questions that help them think about their actions.

"What did you learn from this experience?" or "How do you think you can handle this differently next time?"

Reinforce Love and Support:

Remind them that discipline comes from care, not punishment.

"I'm proud of you, and I want to help you grow into the best version of yourself."

Here's a sample dialogue illustrating how a parent can approach a teenager when addressing a sensitive issue such as the overuse of technology while maintaining respect, understanding, and fostering trust:

Sample Dialogue: Addressing Excessive Screen Time:

Parent:

"Hey, I've been noticing that you spend a lot of time on your phone or computer lately. I want to talk about how you're feeling and see if we can find a balance that works for both of us. Can we chat about this?"

Teenager:

"Yeah, I guess. I just like hanging out online. It's not a big deal."

Parent:

"I understand that you enjoy connecting with your friends and exploring things online—that's important. I just worry about how much time you're spending because it can sometimes make you feel tired or distracted. How do you feel after a long time on your devices?"

Teenager:

"Honestly, I get tired, and my eyes hurt, but I don't want to stop. I feel like I'm missing out if I don't keep up."

Parent:

"That's a really good point. I don't want you to miss out on anything, either, but I also care about your health and focus. Maybe we can figure out some rules together—like no screens an hour before bed or during meals—so you get enough rest and family time. Would you be open to trying that?"

Teenager:

"Maybe. I guess I could try, but I don't want you to take away my phone or make it impossible to talk to my friends."

Parent:

"I'm not here to take everything away or control you. I just want to help you stay healthy and balanced. It's okay to feel frustrated, and I'm here to support you. Let's agree on some limits, and if it doesn't work, we can talk again and adjust. How does that sound?"

Teenager:

"Yeah, I think I can do that. Thanks for listening."

Parent:

"Thank you for being open. I'm proud of you for sharing how you feel. Remember, I'm here to help you grow, and I trust you to make good decisions. We're in this together."

Key Points in This Approach:

Start with understanding and curiosity rather than accusations. Express concerns calmly and focus on health and well-being.

Basic Concept of Respect in a Simple

Involve the teen in decision-making to foster respect and responsibility. Acknowledge their feelings and reassure support.

Plan to revisit the conversation if needed, showing flexibility.

Here's another sample dialogue, this time addressing academic stress or pressure, demonstrating a respectful and supportive approach:

Sample Dialogue: Addressing Academic Stress:

Parent:

"Hey, I noticed you've seemed a little overwhelmed lately with schoolwork. Can we talk about how you're feeling? I want to understand what's going on."

Teenager:

"Yeah, I'm just stressed about all the exams and homework. It's a lot to handle, and I feel like I'm falling behind sometimes."

Parent:

"I hear you. It's completely normal to feel stressed when there's so much going on. School can be tough, and I want you to know I'm here to support you. What do you think is the hardest part right now?"

Teenager:

"Honestly, it's just so much stuff all at once. I don't even know where to start sometimes."

Basic Concept of Respect in a Simple

Parent:

"That's a common feeling, and it's okay to feel overwhelmed. Maybe we can work together to make a plan-like breaking your workload into smaller parts or setting aside specific times for studying. Would you like to try that?"

Teenager:

"Yeah, I think that might help. But I also worry that I won't do well enough, and I don't want to disappoint anyone."

Parent:

"Feeling pressure to succeed is tough, but remember, your best effort is what matters most. Nobody expects perfection. I'm proud of you no matter what, and I believe in your abilities. Let's focus on doing our best and taking care of your health along the way. How about we set some manageable goals together?"

Teenager:

"Okay, I'll try. Thanks for understanding."

Parent:

"Thank you for sharing how you feel. I'm here for you, and I trust you to handle things, just like I trust myself. We'll get through this together, one step at a time."

Key Points in This Approach:

Start with empathetic listening and understanding. Validate their feelings and normalize their stress.

Collaborate on solutions, like planning or time management. Reassure them that effort matters more than perfection.

Reinforce trust and support for their growth.

Here's a short practical guide for parents on how to handle common teenage challenges with respect, patience, and understanding, fostering trust and positive growth:

Parenting Teenagers: A Respectful and Supportive Guide

1. Listen Actively and Empathetically

When your teen shares their feelings or problems, give them your full attention. Maintain eye contact, avoid interrupting, and show genuine interest. Reflect back on what you hear to confirm your understanding. This helps them feel respected and valued, encouraging open communication.

2. Validate Their Emotions

Acknowledge that their feelings are real and valid, even if you don't fully agree. Phrases like, "I understand you're feeling overwhelmed" or "It's okay to feel upset about this" build trust and help them feel safe expressing themselves without fear of judgment.

3. Approach Mistakes as Learning Opportunities

Instead of criticizing, focus on guiding. Use questions like, "What can you learn from this?" or, "How might you handle this differently next time?" This fosters growth and resilience rather than fear of failure.

4. Set Clear, Respectful Boundaries

Establish rules together, screen time limits or curfews, and explain the reasons behind them. Involve your teen in the decision-making process to promote ownership and respect.

Remember, boundaries are about care, not control.

5. Offer Support, Not Ultimatums

When your teen is struggling, offer your help without forcing solutions. Say things like, "I'm here if you want to talk or need help figuring this out," rather than giving orders or making demands. This builds trust and encourages them to seek your guidance when needed.

6. Model the Behavior You Want to See

Show humility, patience, and respect in your own actions. Share your own challenges and how you handle them. Demonstrating self-awareness and vulnerability teaches your teen that making mistakes is part of growth and that seeking help is strong.

7. Be Patient and Consistent

Building trust takes time. Stay consistent in your approach, be patient with their independence, and remember that respect is a two-way street. Your calm, steady presence encourages them to mirror that behavior.

Remember:

Supporting your teen's growth involves understanding their need for independence while guiding them with love, respect, and patience. When they feel truly supported, they are more likely to trust your advice and develop the resilience they need to thrive.

Here's a specific dialogue scenario illustrating how a parent can respectfully and patiently handle a teenage challenge, such as refusing to follow rules about screen time or chores, while fostering trust and understanding:

Scenario: Teen Refuses to Follow Screen Time Rules:

Parent:

"Hey, I noticed you've been on your phone quite a lot today. I understand it's fun and relaxing, but I also want to talk about our agreement on screen time. Can we sit down for a quick chat?"

Teen:

"Yeah, I don't see why I can't just use it whenever I want. It's not a big deal."

Parent:

"I get that you feel that way. I understand how important your devices are for connecting and having fun. I also want to make sure you're getting enough rest and focusing on your other priorities. Can you tell me how you're feeling about the screen limits we agreed on?"

Teen:

"I just think I should have more freedom. Everyone else seems to be doing whatever they want."

Parent:

"I hear you. It's normal to want more freedom, especially as you're growing. My goal is to help you develop healthy habits now that will serve you well in the future. We can review our rules together and see if they still work for you. Maybe we can find a balance that feels fair. How does that sound?"

Teen:

"I guess I can try. But I don't want you to keep checking my stuff or make me feel like I can't trust myself."

Parent:

"That's a good point, and I want to respect your growing independence. I'm not here to check on you all the time or control everything. I trust you to make good choices, and I'm here to support you as you learn. If you ever feel overwhelmed or need to talk, I'm always here. Let's work together on this, okay?"

Teen:

"Okay, I'll try. Thanks for listening."

Parent:

"Thank you for sharing how you feel. I appreciate your honesty. Remember, we're in this together, and I believe in your ability to make smart choices. Let's check in again soon and see how things are going."

Key Takeaways from This Approach:

Start with understanding** rather than confrontation. Respect their feelings** and acknowledge their perspective. Involve them in creating solutions and building ownership.

Reinforce trust by showing you believe in their abilities. Offer ongoing support rather than issuing ultimatums.

Here are additional scenario examples for common teenage challenges, along with respectful, supportive dialogue approaches. These can help you navigate different situations while maintaining trust and fostering positive growth:

Scenario 2: Teen is Falling Behind in School or Losing Motivation

Parent:

"I've noticed you seem a bit less motivated with your schoolwork lately. I want to check in and see how you're feeling about everything. Is there something bothering you or making it hard to focus?"

Teen:

"I just don't see the point anymore. It's too much, and I don't think I can do it all."

Parent:

"I understand that it feels overwhelming sometimes. It's okay to feel like that. Let's talk about what's making it hard. Maybe we can break things into smaller steps or find ways to make studying more interesting. Remember, I believe in your abilities, and I'm here to help you figure out a plan that works for you."

Teen:

"I don't know… I guess I just feel stressed about tests and grades."

Parent:

"That's a common feeling, and it's okay to feel stressed. How about we set a manageable schedule and include some breaks? And if you ever need help studying or understanding something, just ask. You don't have to do this alone. I'm here for you."

Scenario 3: Teen is Making Poor Choices with Friends or Social Media

Parent:

"I've noticed you're spending a lot of time on social media and with certain friends. I want to talk about how that's affecting you. How do you feel about your time online and your friendships?"

Teen:

"They're my friends, and I like hanging out with them. I don't see what's wrong with it."

Parent:

"I get that, and I trust that you're making your own choices.

I just want to make sure you're safe and not getting into situations that might hurt you or make you uncomfortable. Sometimes, social media can be overwhelming or misleading-would you be open to talking about how to use it responsibly?"

Teen:

"Maybe, but I don't want you to tell me what to do."

Parent:

"I understand. I'm not here to tell you what to do, but I care about your safety and happiness. If you ever want to talk about your online life or your friendships, I'm here to listen and support you, not judge. Let's work together to find a balance that feels right for you."

Scenario 4: Teen Resists Family Rules or Traditions

Parent:

"I see that you're feeling frustrated about the rules we've set, like helping out at home or participating in family activities. Can we talk about how you're feeling?"

Teen:

"I just don't think I should have to do all this stuff. I want to do my own thing."

Parent:

"I understand that you want more independence and space. It's natural to want that as you grow. Our rules are here to help you learn responsibility and prepare you for the future. But I also want to hear your thoughts. Is there a way we can make these routines more fair or flexible?"

Teen:

"I guess we could talk about it, but I still don't like doing chores all the time."

Parent:

"Thanks for sharing. Let's figure out a schedule that works for everyone. You can choose which chores to do or set specific times. I trust you to help out, and I want you to feel involved in creating a balance that respects your independence while also caring for our family."

Follow-up Tips to Maintain Trust

Check-in regularly: Follow up on previous conversations to show ongoing support. Acknowledge their efforts: Praise their responsibility and honesty.

Adjust boundaries gradually: Be flexible as they mature and demonstrate responsibility. Keep communication open:

Encourage them to come to you with questions or problems anytime.

Stay calm and patient: Even when disagreements arise, maintain a respectful tone.

Here are specific scripts for common teenage challenges and tips on how to de-escalate conflicts while maintaining respect and trust:

Scripts for Common Challenges

1. Handling Disagreements About Curfew or Bedtime

Parent:

"Hey, I know you're feeling that the curfew is too early tonight. Can we talk about how you're feeling and find a way that works for both of us?"

Teen:

"I don't see why I can't stay out later sometimes. It's not fair."

Parent:

"I hear you. I understand you want more freedom, and I trust you to make good decisions. Let's discuss what a reasonable time might look like and set some guidelines that respect your growing independence. How does that sound?"

2. When Teen Is Using Language or Behavior That Upsets You

Parent:

"I want to talk about how you spoke to me earlier. I felt upset because I wanted us to communicate with respect. Can we discuss what happened?"

Teen:

"I was just annoyed. I didn't mean to upset you."

Parent:

"I understand you're upset, and I appreciate your honesty. I want us to talk openly without feeling hurt or angry. Let's both try to speak kindly, even when we're frustrated. That way, we can better understand each other."

3. When Teen Is Not Engaging in Family Activities

Parent:

"I miss spending time with you during family dinners or outings. How are you feeling about participating in these moments?"

Basic Concept of Respect in a Simple

Teen:

"I don't really want to do it. I have other things to do."

Parent:

"I get it. Sometimes I feel the same way. But I also value our time together because it helps us stay connected. Maybe we can find a balance, like planning some special activities you enjoy. Would you be open to that?"

Tips on How to De-escalate Conflicts Stay Calm:

Keep your voice steady and avoid raising your tone. When you're calm, it's easier for your teen to stay calm, too.

Listen Actively:

Show you're listening by nodding, maintaining eye contact, and summarizing what they say. "So, you're feeling overwhelmed with school and social media, right?"

Validate Feelings:

Acknowledge their emotions without judgment.

"It's understandable to feel frustrated or stressed. I've felt that way too sometimes."

Use "I" Statements:

Express your feelings without blame.

"I feel worried when I see you upset because I care about your well-being."

Offer Solutions, Not Ultimatums:

Suggest together ways to resolve the issue.

"Let's work out a plan that helps you manage your time better. What do you think?"

Take a Break if Needed:

If emotions run high, suggest taking a few minutes to breathe and calm down before continuing the conversation.

Reaffirm Love and Support:

End with a reassurance of your care.

"I love you and want the best for you. We're in this together."

Here are additional scripts tailored for specific issues that teenagers often face, along with respectful, supportive language for parents to foster trust and understanding:

Scripts for Specific Teen Challenges

1. Peer Pressure to Engage in Unhealthy Activities

Basic Concept of Respect in a Simple

Parent:

"I noticed some of your friends are doing things that worry me, like trying substances or risky behavior. Can we talk about how you're feeling about peer pressure?"

Teen:

"They're my friends, and I don't want to lose them. But I don't want to do those things."

Parent:

"I respect that you want to keep your friendships, and I trust you to make the right choices. It's hard when friends encourage us to do things we're unsure about. Remember, true friends respect your boundaries and your feelings. If you ever feel pressured or unsure, you can always come to me. I believe in your ability to stand up for yourself."

2. Teen Struggling with Mental Health or Emotional Well-being

Parent:

"I've noticed you seem more stressed or sad lately. Can we talk about how you're feeling? I want to support you, and I care about your happiness."

Teen:

"I'm just overwhelmed, and I don't want to talk about it."

Parent:

"That's okay. Sometimes, it helps just to know I'm here whenever you're ready. You don't have to handle everything alone. If you want, we can look into talking to someone who can help, like a counselor. Your feelings are important, and I want to support you in feeling better."

3. Teen Wants More Independence, but You're Concerned

Parent:

"I see that you want to do more things on your own, and I'm proud of how you're growing. I also worry sometimes because I want to make sure you're safe. Let's talk about how we can give you more independence while making sure you're protected."

Teen:

"I just want to be treated like an adult."

Parent:

"You are growing into an adult, and I trust you. My goal is

to support you in becoming responsible. How about we set some clear boundaries, like checking in at certain times or setting goals together? That way, you get more freedom, and I feel more comfortable knowing you're okay."

4. Teen Is Not Motivated for Future Goals or Education

Parent:

"I know sometimes it feels like school is a lot, and it's hard to stay motivated. Can we talk about what excites you or what you want for your future?"

Teen:

"I don't really care about school right now. It's boring."

Parent:

"I understand. It's okay to feel that way sometimes. Let's explore what interests you—maybe there's a career or hobby you're passionate about. We can look into ways to help you find purpose and motivation. Remember, I believe in your talents and want to support you in reaching your dreams."

Final Tips for Supportive Conversations

Always listen without interrupting or judging. Validate their feelings, even if you disagree.

Encourage honest dialogue and reassure them of your love. Collaborate on solutions rather than imposing rules.

Be patient. They need time to trust and open up.

Here are specific dialogue templates for common situations, along with tips for effective follow-up to reinforce trust and support:

Dialogue Templates for Common Teen Challenges

1. Peer Pressure and Risky Behavior

Parent:

"Hey, I wanted to talk about something I've noticed. Some of your friends are doing things that worry me, like trying substances or risky activities. How do you feel about that?"

Teen:

"I think they're just having fun. I don't want to do that stuff."

Parent:

"I'm glad you're thinking about it. I trust your judgment, and I want you to know I support you in making safe choices. If you ever feel pressured or unsure, I'm here for you. Remember, real friends respect your boundaries and care about your well-being. Let's keep talking about how you're feeling and what you're comfortable with."

2. Teen Expressing Emotional Struggles

Parent:

"I've noticed you seem upset or stressed lately. Want to talk about how you're feeling? I care about you and want to support you."

Teen:

"I don't really want to talk about it now."

Parent:

"That's okay. You don't have to share everything right now. Just know that I'm here whenever you're ready. If it helps, we could also find someone like a counselor who's trained to support you. Your feelings matter, and I want you to feel safe and cared for."

3. Teens Seeking More Independence

Parent:

"I see you're wanting more freedom and independence, and I'm proud of how you're growing. I also want to make sure you're safe while doing so. How do you think we can find a good balance?"

Teen:

"I just want to do my own thing without so many rules."

Parent:

"That's understandable. I trust you to make responsible choices. How about we set some clear expectations—like checking in at certain times or working towards some goals—and then I can give you more freedom? We can review it regularly, too."

4. Teen Lacking Motivation for School or Goals

Parent:

"I know school can feel boring or overwhelming sometimes. What are some things you're interested in or passionate about? Let's see how we can connect those to your future goals."

Teen:

"I don't really care about school right now."

Parent:

"That's okay. It's normal to feel that way sometimes. Maybe

we can explore some hobbies or ideas that excite you. Remember, I believe in your abilities, and I want to help you find a path that's meaningful for you."

Tips for Effective Follow-Up

Check-in regularly: Follow up on previous conversations, showing ongoing support and interest.

Acknowledge progress: Praise even small efforts or positive changes to reinforce trust.

Be patient and consistent: Trust develops over time through steady, respectful interactions. Encourage ongoing dialogue: Let your teen know that they can always come to you with anything.

Revisit boundaries and goals: Adjust rules as they demonstrate responsibility, showing flexibility and understanding.

Here are sample follow-up conversations and daily check-in suggestions to help you maintain open communication, build trust, and support your teen's growth over time:

Sample Follow-Up Conversations Follow-Up 1: Peer Pressure

Parent:

"Hey, I just wanted to see how you're feeling about the

choices you're making with your friends.

Have you felt any pressure lately, or have things been feeling better?"

Teen:

"Actually, I've been saying no more often, and they're starting to respect that."

Parent:

"That's great to hear! I'm proud of you for standing up for yourself. Remember, I'm here if you ever want to talk or need support. Keep trusting your instincts. You're doing an awesome job."

Follow-Up 2: Emotional Well-being

Parent:

"I've noticed you seem a little calmer lately. How are you feeling now? Do you want to talk about anything that's been on your mind?"

Teen:

"I've been trying to handle things better. It helps when I talk to you or write things down."

Parent:

"I'm really glad to hear that. Keep sharing your feelings. You're not alone. And if you ever feel overwhelmed, we can look into additional support, like talking to someone professionally. I love you and want to see you happy and healthy."

Follow-Up 3: Independence and Boundaries

Parent:

"Last week, we agreed on some new rules about checking in. How's that been going? Do you feel it's working for you?"

Teen:

"Yeah, I think it's okay. It's good to know I can handle some responsibility."

Parent:

"I'm happy to hear that. I trust you to make good decisions, and I'm proud of how responsible you're becoming. Let's keep talking about what's working and make adjustments if needed."

Follow-Up 4: School Motivation

Parent:

"I know you've been feeling a bit stuck with school lately.

Shine Your Light

Have you found anything that excites you or that you want to explore more?"

Teen:

"I've been thinking about trying some new hobbies, like music or art."

Parent:

"That's fantastic! Pursuing your passions can really help motivate you. Let's brainstorm ways to include those interests in your daily routine and see how they can connect to your future goals."

Daily Check-In Suggestions Morning Brief:

Ask, "What are you most excited about today?" or "What's one thing you want to accomplish today?"

This encourages positive focus and helps them set intentions.

Evening Reflection:

Say, "How did your day go? What was the best part?" or "Did anything challenge you today?" This creates space for sharing feelings and recognizing achievements.

Basic Concept of Respect in a Simple

Weekly Review:

Set aside time to discuss progress on goals or boundaries:

"Let's talk about how the rules are working for you this week. Is there anything we should change or improve?"

Express Appreciation:

Regularly tell your teen, "I appreciate your honesty and effort," or "I'm proud of how you handled that situation."

Positive reinforcement builds trust and confidence.

Offer Support:

Remind them, "Remember, I'm always here to listen or help-no matter what." This reassures them they're not alone.

Here's a comprehensive guide on puberty challenges and how parents can support teenagers in understanding and navigating this natural, yet often confusing, phase of growth:

Supporting Teens Through Puberty: Challenges and How to Help Them Grow with Understanding

1.   Recognize Puberty as a Natural Process

Puberty is a vital stage of physical, emotional, and psychological growth. It involves rapid changes - growth spurts, hormonal shifts, emotional fluctuations, and developing new identities. Understanding that these changes are normal helps both parents and teens approach this phase with compassion rather than frustration or confusion.

## 2.	Open and Honest Communication

Create a safe space where your teen feels comfortable talking about their experiences, whether it's about bodily changes, mood swings, or social challenges. Use age-appropriate language and normalize their feelings. For example:

"It's completely normal to feel a bit confused or overwhelmed during these changes. I went through it too, and I'm here for you."

## 3.	Address Physical Changes with Respect and Information

Teenagers often feel embarrassed or awkward about their body changes. Help them understand these changes are part of growing to their full potential. Offer factual, age-appropriate information about:

Body development (growth spurts, acne, hair growth)

Personal hygiene needs

Changes in appetite or sleep patterns

Tip: Have open discussions about hygiene and self-care, emphasizing that caring for their body is a way of respecting themselves.

### 4.	Support Emotional and Mood Fluctuations

Hormonal shifts can cause mood swings, irritability, or feelings of confusion. Validate their emotions:

"It's okay to feel upset or irritable sometimes. These feelings are part of your growth, and I'm here to listen whenever you want to talk."

Encourage healthy outlets for emotional exercise, creative activities, or journaling, and remind them it's okay to seek support if feelings become overwhelming.

### 5.	Respect Their Need for Independence and Identity

Teenagers start exploring their identity, values, and social roles. Respect their desire for independence, but set boundaries that help them feel safe. Use collaborative approaches:

"I trust you to make good choices, but let's also talk about the best ways to handle peer pressure and social situations."

Encourage self-reflection and decision-making, fostering confidence and responsibility.

### 6.	Teach Healthy Boundaries and Relationships

Discuss the importance of respectful relationships, consent, and boundaries, both physical and emotional. Emphasize that these skills are vital for their safety and growth into mature adults.

7. Be Patient and Offer Reassurance

Puberty can be confusing, frustrating, and challenging. Reassure your teen that they are loved unconditionally and that these changes are temporary. Remind them:

"This phase is just part of growing up, and it will pass. You are developing into a strong, capable person."

8. Model Self-Care and Respect

Show your own healthy habits like managing stress, practicing good hygiene, and handling emotions constructively. Your behavior sets a powerful example for your teen to follow.

Summary: How to Help Teenagers Grow with Understanding During Puberty

Normalize physical and emotional changes. Communicate openly and honestly.

Provide age-appropriate information and support.

Respect their need for independence while setting boundaries. Encourage healthy outlets for emotions.

Teach respect in relationships.

Reassure them of your unconditional love. Model self-care and emotional resilience.

Here are conversation starters and activities to help teenagers understand and embrace puberty with openness and positivity:

Conversation Starters for Discussing Puberty

Body Changes

"Hey, I wanted to check in and see how you're feeling about the changes your body is going through. It's all part of growing up, and I'm here to answer any questions you might have."

Emotional Fluctuations

"Sometimes I notice you're feeling really happy or upset, and I want you to know that's okay. Would you like to talk about what's going on inside? I'm here to listen."

Hygiene and Self-Care

"As your body changes, taking care of yourself becomes even more important. Do you want some tips or help with managing your hygiene routines?"

Relationships and Respect

"It's normal to start thinking about relationships and friendships differently. If you want to talk about how to handle those feelings or boundaries, I'm here for you."

Reassuring Growth

"Everyone goes through this phase, and it can feel confusing or awkward. Remember, I went through it too, and it's all part of becoming a strong, confident person."

Activities to Support Understanding and Growth

1.   Body Awareness Journal

Encourage your teen to keep a journal where they write about their feelings, questions, or observations related to their body and emotions. This helps normalize their experience and provides a safe space for reflection.

2.   Self-Care Routine Creation

Work together to develop a personalized self-care routine-showering regularly, skincare, healthy eating, and exercise. Make it fun by choosing products or activities they enjoy.

3.   Educational Videos or Books

Watch age-appropriate videos or read books about puberty

and physical development. Follow up with a discussion about what they learned and any questions that arose.

4. Role-Playing Respectful Relationships

Practice scenarios where they set boundaries or communicate their feelings in relationships. This builds confidence and understanding of healthy interactions.

5. Relaxation and Stress-Relief Activities

Introduce activities like yoga, meditation, or deep breathing exercises to help manage mood swings and stress. Practice together to make it a bonding experience.

6. Celebrate Growth

Create a "Growth Celebration" day where you acknowledge their physical and emotional changes positively. For example, "Today, we celebrate how you're growing into a wonderful young person!"

Here are sample scripts for some of the conversation starters, along with detailed activity ideas to help your teen embrace puberty positively and confidently:

Sample Scripts for Conversations About Puberty

1.   Discussing Body Changes

Parent:

"Hey, I noticed your body is going through some changes, and I want you to know that it's completely normal. Sometimes, it can be confusing or even a little awkward, but I'm here if you have any questions or want to talk about what you're experiencing."

Teen:

"Yeah, I don't really get all the stuff happening."

Parent:

"That's totally okay. It's a lot to process, and everyone goes through it at their own pace. If you ever want to know more or just talk about how you're feeling, I'm always here for you."

2.   Handling Mood Swings or Emotional Changes
Parent:

"I've noticed you've been feeling really up and down lately. That's a normal part of puberty because of hormonal changes. Remember, it's okay to feel all sorts of emotions, sadness and happiness. If you want to talk or need a break, I'm here to listen."

Teen:

"Sometimes I just don't want to talk to anyone."

Parent:

"That's understandable. Take all the time you need. Just know that I love you, and I'm here whenever you're ready to share or if you need anything."

3.   Talking About Hygiene and Self-Care

Parent:

"As your body changes, it's important to take care of yourself, like showering regularly, using deodorant, and paying attention to your skin. Want to go through some tips together or pick out some products you like?"

Teen:

"Yeah, I guess I should start taking better care of myself."

Parent:

"Great! We can make it fun-maybe picking some new soap or skincare products you like. It's all about feeling good and healthy."

4.   Respecting Independence and Identity

Parent:

"I see you're wanting more independence, and I'm proud of how you're growing. Let's talk about how we can give you more space while still making sure you're safe. What do you think would work best?"

Teen:

"I just want to do things on my own, but I also want you to trust me."

Parent:

"I trust you. Let's set some small goals for independence checking in at certain times, and we can revisit and adjust as you grow."

Detailed Activity Ideas

1.   Body Awareness Journal Activity:

Encourage your teen to keep a journal where they write about their feelings, questions, or observations related to their physical and emotional changes.

Basic Concept of Respect in a Simple

Purpose:

Normalizes their experience, helps them process emotions and fosters self-awareness.

2.   Self-Care Routine Creation Activity:

Sit down together and create a personalized self-care plan-this could include daily hygiene, skincare, exercise, and relaxation activities. Let them choose products or activities they enjoy.

Purpose:

Builds independence, self-love, and confidence in caring for their body.

3.   Watch Educational Videos or Read Books Activity:

Find age-appropriate videos or books about puberty and discuss what they learned.

Purpose:

Provides accurate information and reduces misconceptions or fears.

4.   Role-Playing Respectful Boundaries Activity:

Practice scenarios where your teen sets boundaries or communicates feelings in relationships.

Purpose:

Builds confidence in expressing themselves and understanding healthy relationships.

5.   Relaxation and Stress-Relief Practice Activity:

Learn and practice deep breathing, yoga, or meditation together.

Purpose:

Helps manage mood swings, reduces anxiety, and promotes emotional resilience.

6.   Celebrate Growth Day Activity:

Designate a special day to celebrate how your teen is growing physically, emotionally, and spiritually. Do fun activities, share positive affirmations, and acknowledge their journey.

Purpose:

Builds confidence, reinforces positive self-image, and celebrates their unique growth.

Here's a heartfelt and empowering message focused on self-love, gratitude, and community wisdom for teenagers. It encourages self-empowerment and appreciation for parents, teachers, and the community:

Basic Concept of Respect in a Simple

Self-Love, Gratitude, and Community Wisdom for Teenagers

1. Embrace Your Unique Self

Remember, you are a unique and incredible person with your own talents, dreams, and strengths. Practice self-love by celebrating what makes you special: your kindness, creativity, resilience, and curiosity. When you accept and love yourself fully, you become more confident to pursue your goals and stand tall in your truth.

2. Gratitude for Your Parents and Guardians

Take a moment each day to thank your parents or guardians for everything they do, whether it's providing love, support, or guidance. Recognize that their sacrifices and efforts are part of your foundation. Gratitude for their care helps you appreciate the wisdom they pass down and strengthens your bond.

3. Appreciation for Teachers and Mentors

Your teachers and mentors hold a wealth of wisdom that can guide you on your journey. Be thankful for their patience, knowledge, and encouragement. Remember, every lesson they teach is a gift that helps shape your future. Show appreciation through kind words, gratitude, or simply listening with an open heart.

4.   Recognize the Wisdom in Your Community

Every community has collective wisdom stories, traditions, and lessons passed down through generations. Be open to learning from those around you. Respect and honor elders' experiences, and seek their guidance when you're unsure. This helps you stay grounded and connected to your roots.

5.   Empower Yourself with Inner Strength

Believe in your power to create positive change within yourself and in the world. Practice affirmations like:

"I am worthy of love and success,"

"I am capable of overcoming challenges," and "My voice is important."

These affirmations reinforce your self-worth and help you grow into a confident, compassionate leader.

6.   Cultivate Gratitude and Compassion

Express gratitude not only for what you receive but also for what you can give kindness, understanding, and support to others. When you cultivate gratitude, you attract more positivity and love into your life. Remember, gratitude is a powerful tool for self-empowerment and community building.

7. Be a Light for Others

As you love and appreciate yourself, share that light with

those around you. Lift others up with encouraging words, acts of kindness, and support. When we lift each other, the entire community grows stronger and wiser.

8.   Trust Your Inner Wisdom

Know that within you lies divine wisdom, your intuition, and the voice that guides you. Trust yourself to make decisions aligned with your highest good. The more you listen to your inner voice, the more empowered and confident you become.

Affirmation for Self-Love and Gratitude

"I am worthy of love, respect, and happiness. I honor my journey, embrace my uniqueness, and celebrate my growth. I am grateful for my parents, teachers, and community. They are my guiding lights. Together, we grow stronger in love, wisdom, and unity."

Here's a powerful, compassionate message aimed at parents and teachers, offering guidance on nurturing respect, emotional understanding, and discipline in children, especially in today's busy world:

Shine Your Light

A Message to Parents and Teachers: Nurturing Respect and Emotional Wisdom in Children

Dear Parents and Educators,

In our busy lives, it's easy to become caught up in work responsibilities, and don't ever forget to tell your children you love them every time they leave the house and daily routines, often leaving little time for meaningful connection with your children. Yet, the greatest gift we can give them is not only education but also the wisdom of emotional understanding, respect, and discipline rooted in love.

Children are like tender seeds. They need nurturing, patience, and guidance. Many young minds today are self-centered because they have not yet learned to understand their own emotions or those of others. This is a natural part of growth, but it requires our conscious effort to nurture empathy, respect, and emotional intelligence within them.

As adults, our role is to model these qualities daily. Show kindness, listen actively, and validate their feelings. When children see respect and compassion in their environment, they learn to mirror those behaviors. Discipline rooted in love and understanding rather than punishment teaches them to recognize boundaries, develop self-control, and respect the feelings of others.

Remember, discipline is not about control but about guiding children to discover their inner strength and responsibility. Use patience, set clear boundaries, and communicate with kindness. When children make mistakes, instead of blaming them, help them understand what they can do differently next time, fostering growth and resilience.

Basic Concept of Respect in a Simple

For parents and teachers alike, taking a few moments each day to connect deeply with children listening to their fears, dreams, and frustrations can transform their understanding of themselves and others. It's during these moments of genuine connection that seeds of emotional wisdom are planted.

Let's encourage children to express their feelings safely and openly. Teach them that emotions are natural and that respecting others' feelings is a sign of strength. Celebrate acts of kindness and empathy, and gently guide them back when they stray into selfishness or disrespect.

In this shared journey, remember that patience, love, and consistency are our most powerful tools. When we invest time and energy into fostering emotional intelligence and respect, we're laying the foundation for a generation that is compassionate, responsible, and wise.

Together, let's nurture respectful hearts and understanding minds, creating a future where kindness and wisdom flourish.

A Short Daily Reminder for Parents and Teachers:

"Every moment is an opportunity to teach love, respect, and understanding. Through patience and kindness, we plant seeds of wisdom that will grow into a brighter future."

Shine Your Light

Here are specific activities and daily practices for parents and teachers to help nurture respect, emotional understanding, and discipline in children, inspired by the message above:

Activities and Daily Practices for Parents and Teachers

1.   Daily Reflection and Gratitude Circle Activity:

Set aside 5-10 minutes each day for children to share one thing they are grateful for and one act of kindness they did or received.

Purpose:

Encourages gratitude, self-awareness, and recognition of kindness, fostering respect and emotional connection.

2.   Empathy Role-Play Activity:

Create simple scenarios where children practice expressing their feelings and understanding others' emotions. For example, "How would you feel if someone took your toy without asking?" Purpose:

Builds emotional intelligence and respect by encouraging children to see situations from others' perspectives.

3.   Kindness Challenge Activity:

Challenge children to perform one act of kindness each day,

helping a sibling, sharing with friends, or saying something nice to someone.

Purpose:

Reinforces positive social behaviors and respect for others.

4.   Mindful Listening Practice Activity:

Teach children to practice active listening, looking into the speaker's eyes, not interrupting, and summarizing what they hear.

Purpose:

Develops respect, patience, and emotional understanding.

5.   Respect and Discipline Chart Activity:

Create a visual chart where children earn stars or points for respectful behavior, kindness, and self-control. Rewards can be simple, like choosing a game or extra story time.

Purpose:

Encourages responsibility and positive discipline through recognition and reinforcement.

6.   Emotional Check-In Journal Activity:

Encourage children to write or draw about how they're feeling each day. Parents and teachers can review these gently to understand their emotional state.

Purpose:

Fosters emotional awareness and helps children learn to express their feelings healthily.

7.   Family or Class "Respect Pledge" Activity:

Create a simple pledge about respecting others, listening, and kindness. Have children and adults sign it and display it prominently.

Purpose:

Builds a shared commitment to respectful behavior and community values.

8.   Celebrate Acts of Compassion Activity:

Regularly highlight and praise children when they show kindness, respect, or empathy. Share stories of their good deeds with others.

Purpose:

Reinforces positive behavior and encourages children to continue practicing respect and kindness.

Basic Concept of Respect in a Simple

Here's a motivational speech designed to inspire parents and teachers to actively nurture respect, emotional intelligence, and discipline in children, fostering a caring and responsible generation:

Motivational Speech for Parents and Teachers: Cultivating Respect and Wisdom in Children

Dear Parents and Educators,

Today, I want to remind us all of the incredible power we hold the power to shape hearts, minds, and spirits. Every day, in our words, actions, and choices, we are planting seeds of respect, kindness, and wisdom in the young minds before us.

Our children are like delicate seeds; they need patience, love, and guidance to grow into strong, compassionate individuals. In this fast-paced world, it's easy to overlook the importance of emotional understanding and respect, yet these qualities are the foundation of a harmonious society.

We live in a time where children are often immersed in screens and distractions, making it more vital than ever to consciously teach them the value of empathy, patience, and discipline. It's not enough to simply instruct; we must model respectful behavior ourselves. When we listen deeply, speak kindly, and act with integrity, children learn by example.

Every act of kindness we show them, every moment of patience, and every lesson of responsibility we impart are the true gifts. When children experience genuine love and respect, they develop self-love and confidence, becoming responsible beings capable of creating positive change.

Shine Your Light

Remember, a discipline rooted in love and understanding teaches responsibility without shame. It guides children to discover their inner strength and integrity rather than instilling fear or resentment. When they stumble, let's help them learn, grow, and try again, fostering resilience and humility.

Together, let's commit to nurturing a generation that respects themselves, others, and the world around them. Because when we invest in their emotional wisdom today, we build a brighter, more compassionate tomorrow.

Let us be the guiding light, planting seeds of respect, kindness, and wisdom that will blossom into a future filled with love and understanding.

Thank you.

Basic Concept of Respect in a Simple

Here are short inspirational quotes and daily affirmations for parents and teachers to reinforce the importance of nurturing respect, kindness, and wisdom in children:

Inspirational Quotes for Parents and Teachers

"The way we treat our children is the foundation of a respectful and compassionate world." "Every act of kindness we show today plants a seed for a brighter tomorrow."

"Children learn more from what we are than what we teach." W.E. Deming: "Teaching respect is planting a garden of love that grows forever."

"The greatest gift you can give a child is your time, patience, and understanding."

"Empower children with kindness, and watch them grow into leaders of love."

"In every child's heart is the potential for greatness and nurture it with respect and compassion." "Discipline rooted in love guides children to discover their inner strength."

"Respect is the bridge that connects hearts and builds peaceful communities." "When children feel valued and understood, they blossom into their best selves."

Shine Your Light

Daily Affirmations for Parents and Teachers

"Today, I choose patience, kindness, and understanding in my interactions." "I am a positive role model of respect, love, and wisdom."

"Every moment is an opportunity to teach and inspire compassion." "I trust in the innate goodness and potential of every child."

"My words and actions plant seeds of hope and confidence." "I am patient and gentle as I guide children to learn and grow." "Today, I will listen deeply and speak kindly."

"I believe in the power of love and respect to transform lives."

"I am committed to creating a safe and nurturing space for all children." "Every child is a gift, and I honor their unique journey."

I am sharing a heartfelt concern. Addressing bullying rooted in deep emotional pain requires compassion, understanding, and a community effort. Here's a thoughtful approach to helping society, schools, and parents understand the root causes, foster empathy, and create a nurturing environment for all children, especially those who bully because they're hurting inside:

Basic Concept of Respect in a Simple

Understanding and Addressing Bullying: A Compassionate Approach

1.   Recognize the Root Causes of Bullying

Many children who bully others are often struggling with their own feelings of hurt, rejection, or loneliness. They might lack love, care, or emotional support at home or school, leading them to act out as a way to feel empowered or to mask their pain. It's crucial for parents, teachers, and communities to see bullying not just as bad behavior but as a cry for help from a wounded heart.

2.   Foster Open Communication and Emotional Expression

Create safe spaces where children feel comfortable sharing their feelings without fear of judgment. Encourage them to talk about their insecurities, fears, or frustrations. Use questions like:

"How are you feeling today?"

"Is there something bothering you that you want to share?"
"What makes you happy or sad?"

When children are heard and understood, they're less likely to lash out at others.

3.   Approach Bullying with Empathy and Compassion

When addressing bullying incidents, instead of punishment alone, guide children, both victims and bullies with kindness. For the bully, say:

"I see you might be feeling upset or insecure. Would you like to talk about what's bothering you?"

"Sometimes, we act out because we're hurting inside. How can I support you?"

For victims, reassure them that their feelings are valid and that they are not alone. Teach children that everyone has feelings and that understanding each other's emotions fosters kindness and respect.

4.   Promote Emotional Literacy and Self-awareness

Teach children to identify and name their emotions, anger, sadness, fear, or insecurity and to express them constructively. Practice activities like journaling, role-playing, or mindfulness to help children understand themselves better and develop empathy for others.

Example: "When you feel angry, take a deep breath and tell yourself it's okay to feel that way. Then, talk about what's bothering you with someone you trust."

5.   Encourage Peer Support and Positive Role Models

In schools, develop programs where children can learn about

empathy, kindness, and conflict resolution. Celebrate acts of compassion and teamwork. Peer mentoring can also help children who feel insecure learn to express themselves positively and build confidence.

6.   Facilitate Respectful Conversations Between Parents and Schools

When conflicts or bullying incidents occur, parents and teachers should meet with a mindset rooted in understanding rather than blame. Approach the situation with questions like: "What do you think might be causing this behavior?"

"How can we work together to support the children involved?"

"What kind of activities can help foster empathy and emotional understanding?"

Focus on creating solutions that include emotional support, counseling, and community-building activities.

7.   Teach Self-Worth and Self-Compassion

Help children build a positive self-image through affirmations, talents, and supportive relationships. When children feel loved and valued, they're less likely to seek validation through bullying or negative behavior.

Shine Your Light

Summary: Building a Compassionate Community

Understand that behind bullying is often pain and insecurity. Create safe spaces for children to express their feelings.

Approach bullies with kindness and empathy, guiding them to express their emotions constructively.

Encourage emotional literacy, self-awareness, and peer support.

Foster open dialogue between parents, teachers, and children, focusing on solutions and understanding.

Build a community where love, respect, and compassion are the guiding principles.

Here are specific dialogues for teachers and parents to approach bullying with kindness and empathy, along with activities to help children develop emotional awareness and compassion.

Sample Dialogues for Addressing Bullying with Kindness and Empathy

1.   Approaching a Child Who Is Bullying Teacher/Parent:

"I noticed you were upset earlier, and it seemed like you acted out toward your classmate. Sometimes, people act out because they're feeling hurt or insecure inside. Would you like to talk about what's bothering you?"

Basic Concept of Respect in a Simple

Child:

"I'm just mad at them because they're better at sports than me."

Teacher/Parent:

"It's okay to feel upset about that. Everyone has strengths and things they're working on. Sometimes, when we feel insecure, we try to put others down. But I believe you're a kind person, and I want to help you feel good about yourself. Let's talk about what makes you feel confident."

2.   Supporting a Victim Teacher/Parent:

"I'm sorry you felt hurt by what happened. Your feelings are important, and it's okay to be upset.

Remember, you don't have to face this alone. If you ever want to talk or need help, I'm here for you."

Child:

"I just want it to stop."

Teacher/Parent:

"I understand, and we're going to work together to make sure you feel safe. Let's also think about ways to express your feelings calmly and confidently so your voice is heard."

3.   Helping a Child Express Emotions

Teacher/Parent:

"Sometimes, it helps to tell me how you're feeling inside.

Shine Your Light

Can you try to name the emotion you're experiencing right now? Are you angry, sad, scared, or something else?"

Child:

"I guess I'm just really upset."

Teacher/Parent:

"That's okay. It's good to recognize how you feel. When you know your emotions, you can share them in a way that helps others understand you. Let's practice saying, 'I feel sad because...' or 'I feel angry when...'"

Activities to Build Empathy and Emotional Awareness

1.   Feelings Chart and Sharing Circle Activity:

Create a chart with different emotions (happy, sad, angry, scared, excited). Have children choose an emotion they've felt during the day and share a story about it.

Purpose:

Helps children identify and articulate their feelings and learn to listen to others.

2.   The Empathy Walk Activity:

Pair children and assign each to walk a few steps in each other's shoes. One child shares a worry or feeling, and the other responds with understanding and support. Switch roles.

Purpose:

Builds empathy by experiencing others' perspectives.

3.   Kindness Challenge Chart Activity:

Encourage children to perform one act of kindness daily—such as complimenting a peer, helping with chores, or sharing a toy—and record their acts on a chart. Celebrate their efforts weekly.

Purpose:

Reinforces positive social behavior and self-awareness.

4.   Emotion Journaling Activity:

Encourage children to keep a journal where they write or draw how they felt during specific situations. Review entries together to discuss feelings and responses.

Purpose:

Fosters emotional literacy and self-reflection.

5.   Role-Playing Conflict Resolution Activity:

Create scenarios where children practice resolving conflicts respectfully—listening, expressing feelings calmly, and finding solutions.

Shine Your Light

Purpose:

Teaches effective communication and empathy in real situations.

Here's a detailed lesson plan designed to help teachers and parents implement activities that foster empathy, emotional awareness, and respectful communication in children. It includes objectives, materials, step-by-step instructions, and reflection questions.

Lesson Plan: Building Empathy and Respect in Children Objective:

To help children recognize and express their emotions.

To develop empathy by understanding others' feelings.

To promote respectful communication and conflict resolution.

Materials Needed:

Feelings chart (with emotions like happy, sad, angry, scared, excited) Journals or paper and coloring supplies

Scenario cards for role-playing Chart or poster for kindness act Stickers or stars for reward system Timer or clock

Lesson Duration:

45-60 minutes

Part 1: Feelings Recognition and Sharing (15 minutes)

Basic Concept of Respect in a Simple

Activity Steps:

Introduction (5 mins):

Explain that everyone experiences different feelings and that understanding our emotions helps us communicate better and connect with others.

Feelings Chart Activity (10 mins):

Show children the feelings chart.

Ask each child to pick an emotion they felt today or recently. Invite them to share a short story about when they felt that way. Encourage active listening and respectful responses from peers.

Reflection Questions:

How do you feel when someone understands your feelings? Why is it important to recognize our emotions?

Part 2: Empathy Walk (15 minutes)

Activity Steps:

Pair children up.

Explain the activity: One child will share a worry or feeling, and the other will respond with understanding and support. Then, switch roles.

Set a timer (2-3 minutes per person). Debrief:

Ask children how it felt to share or listen.

Discuss how understanding others' feelings can help us become kinder friends.

Reflection Questions:

What did you learn about your partner's feelings? How does it feel to be understood?

Part 3: Kindness Acts and Journaling (10 minutes) Activity Steps:

Kindness Challenge Chart:

Explain that today, they will perform one act of kindness.

Write or draw acts on a chart or poster as they do them during the week. Emotion Journaling:

Give each child a journal or paper.

Invite them to draw or write about a time they felt happy, sad, or upset. Encourage sharing if they feel comfortable.

Reflection Questions:

What makes you feel loved or appreciated? How can kindness change how we feel?

Part 4: Conflict Resolution Role-Playing (15 minutes) Activity Steps:

Introduce common conflict scenarios (e.g., someone taking a toy without asking or teasing).

Basic Concept of Respect in a Simple

Role-play:

Assign roles (the person who is upset, the person who caused the upset). Practice respectful ways to express feelings and find solutions.

Discuss:

What worked well?

How did it feel to speak calmly and listen?

Reflection Questions:

What did you learn about expressing your feelings? How can you solve conflicts kindly?

Closing and Reflection (5 minutes):

Summarize key points about empathy, respect, and kindness.

Reinforce that understanding our feelings and others' feelings helps us create a caring community.

Celebrate children's efforts with stickers or stars for participation and kindness.

Follow-Up:

Repeat these activities regularly.

Celebrate acts of kindness and emotional sharing.

Encourage children to practice these skills at home and in their communities.

Absolutely! Here are handouts and activity sheets that you can print and use to reinforce the lessons on empathy, respect, and emotional awareness. These tools are designed to be engaging and easy to incorporate into your classroom or home activities.

Handout 1: Feelings and Emotions Chart Title: Understanding Our Feelings Instructions:

Look at the chart below. Think about a time you felt each emotion. Draw a picture or write a

sentence about that moment.

Emotion	What Makes You Feel This Way?	Your Example (Optional)
Happy		
Sad		
Angry		
Scared		
Excited		

Goal:

Help children recognize and name their feelings to foster emotional literacy. Handout 2: Empathy Role-Play Scenarios

Title: Practice Empathy

Basic Concept of Respect in a Simple

Instructions:

In pairs, take turns acting out these scenarios. After each, talk about what the other person might be feeling.

Scenario 1:

Someone took your favorite toy without asking. How do you feel? What can you say?

Scenario 2:

Your friend is crying because they lost their pet. What can you do or say to help?

Scenario 3:

A classmate looks upset but doesn't want to talk. How can you show you care?

Discussion Questions:

How do you think the other person feels? What kind of words or actions can help?

Activity Sheet: Kindness Challenge Tracker Title: Acts of Kindness

Instructions:

Each day, do one kind of thing for someone. Write or draw

Shine Your Light

what you did!

Day	Kind Act You Did	How Did It Make You Feel?
Monday		
Tuesday		
Wednesday		
Thursday		
Friday		

Encouragement:

Be a kind hero! Small acts can change the world. Printable Conflict Resolution Script

Title: Talking Calmly When We Disagree

Instructions:

Use these sentences to help you talk kindly when you're upset.

"I feel upset because..." "Can you please...?"

"Let's find a solution together." "Thank you for listening."

Example:

"I feel upset because you took my book without asking. Can you please ask next time? Let's find a way to share nicely."

Basic Concept of Respect in a Simple

Printable Resources for Teachers and Parents

1.   Kindness Certificate of Appreciation Purpose:

Encourage children to perform acts of kindness and recognize their efforts.

Design:

A colorful certificate with space for their name and the act of kindness they performed.

Certificate Text:

"Kindness Superstar Award" This certificate is awarded to [Child's Name]

for demonstrating kindness, empathy, and caring in our community. Keep shining your light!

Date: _

(Optional: Add space for signatures of teachers or parents)

2.   Respect and Empathy Poster Design:

A bright poster with simple, memorable tips.

Content:

"How to Show Respect and Kindness" Listen carefully when others speak.

Say kind words and use gentle actions.

Shine Your Light

Try to see things from someone else's point of view. Say "please" and "thank you."

Help others when they need it. Be patient and forgiving.

(Add colorful illustrations or icons for each tip)

3.   Conflict Resolution Step-by-Step Chart Design:

A visual guide with simple steps children can follow when resolving conflicts.

Content:

"How to Solve Problems Kindly" Take a deep breath.

Use respectful words. Say how you feel.

Listen to the other person. Find a solution together.

Say "thank you" for listening.

(Add space for children to write or draw their own solutions)

4.   Daily Reflection Journal Page Design:

A page with prompts to help children reflect on their feelings and actions each day.

Prompts:

Today, I felt _ because _. I showed kindness by.

Something I learned about myself today is. Tomorrow, I want to try.

(Encourage drawing or writing)

5.   Parent-Teacher Communication Log Purpose:

A simple sheet for sharing observations and goals.

Content:

"Weekly Reflection" Child's Name:

What I saw this week:

What the child is doing well:

Goals for next week:

Notes or comments:

(Use for ongoing communication and consistency)

Here's a heartfelt and inspiring message tailored for new parents, emphasizing their vital role in nurturing respect, love, and emotional wisdom in their children from the very beginning:

Message for New Parents: Nurturing a Foundation of Love and Respect

Dear New Parents,

Congratulations on embarking on one of life's most precious journeys, raising a new life filled with potential, dreams, and endless possibilities. As you begin this incredible chapter, remember that your love, patience, and guidance are the foundation upon which your child will build their future.

Every moment you spend nurturing their emotional well-being, teaching kindness, and modeling respect shapes their understanding of how to relate to others. Children are like delicate seeds; they thrive when they feel safe, loved, and valued. By showing them empathy and gratitude every day, you help cultivate their inner strength, compassion, and confidence.

Understand that your child is not just learning words or behaviors. They are absorbing your attitudes and values. Your actions speak louder than words. When you listen attentively, speak kindly, and express appreciation, you set an example that will guide them for a lifetime.

Basic Concept of Respect in a Simple

Remember, parenting is a journey of continuous growth for you and your child. Embrace patience and humility, knowing that mistakes are part of learning. Celebrate small victories like a kind word, a shared smile, or a moment of understanding, and cherish the beautiful process of watching your child blossom into their best self.

Above all, trust in the love you give and the wisdom you nurture. Your gentle guidance, rooted in respect and compassion, will help your child develop into a wise, kind, and confident individual capable of creating a brighter, more loving world.

With love and gratitude,

You are the greatest gift your child will ever receive.

Lesson for New Parents with Toddlers: The Power of Presence and Gentle Guidance

1.   Toddlers don't need perfection. They need presence.

At this stage, your calm presence matters more than any perfect parenting technique. Toddlers are sensitive, curious, and full of raw emotions. They won't always understand your words, but they always feel your energy. Slow down, kneel to their eye level, and let them feel your love through your tone, touch, and attention.

2.   Teach through example, not just words.

Toddlers absorb everything. They learn how to express gratitude, respect, and kindness by *watching* how you treat them and others. When they see, you say "thank you," use gentle words, and respect their needs, they begin to mirror those same habits.

3.   Big emotions are normal.

Your toddler will scream, cry, hit, and push boundaries. This isn't "bad behavior". It's undeveloped emotional regulation. Instead of reacting with anger, take a breath and help them name their feelings: "You're feeling mad because you didn't get what you wanted." Labeling emotions helps them feel seen and teaches emotional vocabulary early.

4.   Create peaceful rituals.

Simple routines like morning cuddles, nighttime gratitude prayers, or saying "thank you" together after meals build security and values. These little habits plant seeds of love, faith, and gratitude that grow with them.

**5.	Respect starts small.**

Respect for elders and parents begins with how *you* respect your toddler. Ask for cooperation instead of demanding. Explain decisions at their level. Say "please" and "thank you" to them. When they feel respected, they naturally learn to offer it to others.

**6.	Nurture their independence.**

Give toddlers choices where possible: "Do you want to wear the red shirt or blue?" This helps them feel empowered and reduces tantrums. It also shows respect for their developing identity.

**7.	Your regulation teaches theirs.**

When they're overwhelmed, your calm voice and steady tone help regulate their nervous system. Breathe deeply, speak slowly, and be calm in their storm. You are their emotional anchor.

**8.	Set boundaries with love.**

It's okay to say "no," but how you say it matters. Use warm firmness: "I can't let you hit, even when you're upset. Let's try stomping or using our words instead." Boundaries create safety and teach self-control.

**9.	Celebrate small acts of kindness.**

When your toddler shares, says "thank you," or helps, praise gently: "That was so kind!" This reinforces gratitude and empathy as natural parts of life.

10.   Be gentle with yourself.

You're learning, too. There will be tears (yours and theirs). Grace matters. Forgive yourself, apologize when needed, and model the very compassion you want your child to learn.

Here's a heartfelt and inspiring message for kids and students in middle age (roughly ages 10-15), emphasizing their potential, responsibility, and the importance of respect, self-love, and kindness:

Message for Kids and Middle School Students: Embrace Your Power, Dear Young Souls,

You are at a special stage of life, a time of discovery, growth, and endless potential. Remember, within you lies a powerful spark of greatness waiting to shine. Every choice you make shapes who you become, so choose kindness, respect, and love for yourself and others.

Respect isn't just about manners; it's about recognizing the values and feelings of everyone around you. When you listen and show appreciation, you create bonds of trust and friendship that can last a lifetime. Be proud of your uniqueness, and don't let anyone's words or actions dim your light. You are capable of achieving incredible things when you believe in yourself.

Mistakes and challenges are part of your journey; they help you learn, grow stronger, and discover your true potential. Every day offers a new opportunity to be kind, brave, and honest. Remember, your actions can inspire others to do the same.

Stay curious, keep learning, and always strive to be the best version of yourself. You are the future bright, compassionate, and full of possibilities. Trust in your inner wisdom, nurture your dreams, and know that the world needs your kindness and your light.

You are loved. You are powerful. You are capable of creating a better tomorrow.

Message for the School Principal: Leading with Wisdom and Compassion Dear Esteemed Principal,

As the guiding force of your school, your leadership sets the tone for a nurturing, respectful, and inspiring environment. Your dedication to fostering not just academic excellence but also character-building creates a legacy that impacts generations.

Your compassion, wisdom, and unwavering commitment to the well-being of students and staff alike are the pillars that uphold a thriving school community. By leading with kindness and understanding, you nurture young minds to develop respect, empathy, and confidence—values that will serve them throughout their lives.

In every decision you make, remember that you are shaping future leaders who will carry forward the principles of love, respect, and responsibility. Your role is vital in creating a safe space where students feel valued, supported, and inspired to reach their highest potential.

Thank you for your inspiring leadership and for believing in the power of education to transform lives. Together, with your guidance, we can cultivate a generation of compassionate, wise, and empowered individuals who will build a brighter future for all.

With heartfelt respect and appreciation,

Your Partner in Education

Here's a heartfelt and inspiring message for teachers, emphasizing their vital role, compassion, and the impact they have on shaping young lives:

Message for Teachers: Honoring Your Dedication and Impact

Dear Teachers,

You are the architects of the future, the gentle guiding hands shaping young minds and hearts. Every lesson you teach, every moment of patience you offer, and every act of kindness you extend leave a lasting imprint on your students' lives. Your dedication goes beyond textbooks and tests; it's about inspiring confidence, fostering respect, and nurturing the innate potential within each child.

In a world full of distractions and challenges, your compassion and commitment are the light that helps students find their way. When you listen with an open heart, you teach them the importance of understanding and empathy. When you believe in their abilities, you empower them to believe in themselves.

Remember, your work is a sacred calling, transforming lives one lesson, one smile, and one act of kindness at a time. Your efforts plant seeds of wisdom, patience, and love that will grow into future leaders and compassionate citizens.

Thank you for your unwavering dedication, your inspiring spirit, and for being a beacon of hope and wisdom. Together, with your guidance, we are creating a generation that values respect, kindness, and continuous growth.

With deep appreciation and respect,

Your Fellow Changemakers in Education

Message for Teenage Parents: Embracing Your Strength and Responsibility

Dear Teenage Parents,

You are embarking on a journey filled with love, strength, and incredible responsibility. While it may come with challenges, remember that your courage and dedication are the foundation for your child's future. Every moment you spend nurturing their growth through kindness, patience, and understanding plants seeds of confidence, respect, and resilience that will serve them for a lifetime.

Parenting at a young age is no easy task, but your love and commitment can overcome obstacles and create a positive, nurturing environment. Embrace your role with humility, knowing that your efforts to listen, support, and guide your child with compassion are the greatest gifts you can give.

Your child looks up to you as their first teacher of kindness, respect, and hope. By showing them love and respect, you teach them how to treat others and build strong, healthy relationships.

Remember, you are not alone; reach out for support, share

your experiences, and trust in your ability to nurture a bright future for your family.

You are strong, capable, and deeply important. Your journey may have its hurdles, but your love and perseverance will shape a generation of compassionate, confident, and respectful individuals. With heartfelt admiration and support,

You Are the Heart of Their Future.

Here's a thoughtful and compassionate message for children who see themselves as bullies, emphasizing understanding, self-awareness, and the possibility of positive change:

Message for Kids Who See Themselves as Bullies: A Path to Growth and Kindness

Dear Young Friend,

If you see yourself as someone who has hurt others or acted mean, remember that everyone makes mistakes—what matters most is what you choose to do next. Deep inside, you have a kind and strong heart, and recognizing the hurt you've caused is the first step toward making positive changes.

You might be acting out because you're feeling upset, insecure, or lonely inside. Sometimes, when we don't know how to express our feelings, we hurt others to feel a little better about ourselves. But you have the power to change that. You can choose kindness, understanding, and respect.

Start by forgiving yourself for past actions and believing that you can become a better person. When you show kindness to others, you not only help them but also help yourself feel happier and more confident. Remember, every kind word or act is a step toward healing your heart and building strong, respectful relationships.

You have the strength to grow into someone who lifts others up instead of bringing them down. Believe in your ability to change, and don't be afraid to ask for help or talk about how you're feeling. You are capable of creating a brighter, kinder future—for yourself and those around you.

You are not alone, and everyone deserves a second chance. Your kindness can transform your life and the lives of others.

Here's a short, encouraging message for children who see themselves as bullies, emphasizing hope and the possibility of positive change:

Short Message for Kids Who See Themselves as Bullies

Dear Friend,

If you've hurt others or acted mean, remember that everyone makes mistakes. The good news is you have the power to change. Inside you are kindness and strength—sometimes, you just need to believe in yourself.

You can start by forgiving yourself and choosing to be kind today. Even small acts of kindness can make a big difference—both for others and for how you feel inside. You are capable of becoming someone who lifts others up and creates happiness.

Believe in your ability to grow and be better. Everyone

deserves a second chance, including you. The path to kindness begins with one step—take it today.

Here are practical steps and affirmations to help children who see themselves as bullies take positive actions and build self-belief:

Practical Steps for Positive Change: Reflect and Acknowledge

Encourage the child to think about times they hurt others and understand how it made others feel. Writing or talking about these feelings helps them become aware and responsible.

Apologize and Make Amends

Teach them the importance of sincerely apologizing to anyone they've hurt. Making amends shows humility and a genuine desire to change.

Practice Kindness Daily

Set small goals, like complimenting someone, sharing, or helping a classmate. Consistent acts of kindness build new habits and feelings of inner strength.

Express Feelings Constructively

Help them find healthy ways to express their emotions—like drawing, talking to a trusted adult, or journaling—so they don't act out in hurtful ways.

Seek Support and Guidance

Encourage talking to a teacher, counselor, or parent when feeling upset or insecure. Supportive adults can provide tools to manage emotions and develop empathy.

Create a Kindness Journal

Have them record daily acts of kindness or moments when they felt proud of themselves. Celebrate these successes to reinforce positive behavior.

Set Personal Goals

Help them set achievable goals like "I will say something nice to three classmates today." Small steps lead to big changes over time.

Positive Affirmations to Build Self-Belief

"I am capable of kindness and good choices." "Every day, I grow stronger and more caring."

"I forgive myself and am ready to make better choices." "I can be someone who lifts others up."

"I believe in my ability to change and grow." "My kindness makes me a better person."

"Today is a new day to be better than yesterday."

Shine Your Light

Here a motivational stories and additional activities to reinforce the message of positive change, kindness, and self-belief for children who want to grow beyond their past actions:

Motivational Story: The Seed of Kindness

Once upon a time, there was a young tree named Leo who often felt angry and lonely. Instead of talking to others, Leo would sometimes push or tease the smaller plants around him. One day, a wise old owl saw Leo acting out and asked, "Why do you behave this way?"

Leo sighed and said, "I feel invisible and angry inside. I don't know how to deal with my feelings." The owl smiled gently and said, "Every seed has the power to grow into something beautiful. When you plant kindness instead of anger, your roots will grow deep, and you'll become strong and loved."

Leo decided to try. Every day, he complimented the flowers, shared his shade with smaller plants, and apologized when he made mistakes. Slowly, Leo's heart filled with warmth, and he saw how much happier everyone was around him.

From that day on, Leo learned that kindness is the true strength, and every small act can grow into something magnificent. And just like Leo, you too can choose kindness and watch yourself bloom into someone truly extraordinary.

Activities to Reinforce Growth and Kindness

Basic Concept of Respect in a Simple

1.   Kindness Chain:

Each day, children write or draw one act of kindness they did or saw someone do. Connect these acts in a chain on a wall or bulletin board. Over time, this visual reminder helps reinforce their power to make a difference.

2.   "If I Were a Hero" Drawing:

Ask children to draw themselves as a kindness hero—saving someone, helping a friend, or planting kindness in their community. Have them share their drawings and stories to inspire others.

3.   Feelings Balloon:

Give children a paper balloon. They write or draw their feelings, anger, sadness, happiness, inside it. Then, discuss ways to "pop" the balloon safely, like talking to someone, taking deep breaths, or doing a calming activity.

4.   Compliment Day:

Set a day where children give genuine compliments to classmates or family members. Encourage them to notice and say nice things about others' strengths or efforts.

5.   Gratitude Letter:

Shine Your Light

Have children write a letter to someone they appreciate—parents, teachers, friends—and share how that person has helped them grow. This deepens gratitude and respect.

Here's a heartfelt and respectful message tailored for school bus drivers, recognizing their vital role in caring for children and ensuring their safety:

Message for School Bus Drivers: Guardians of Safety and Smiles

Dear School Bus Drivers,

Thank you for being more than just drivers—you are the warm, caring guardians who greet children every morning and send them off every afternoon. Your role is incredibly important, as you not only transport students safely but also create a positive, nurturing environment that sets the tone for their day.

Every smile, kind word, and gentle gesture you offer helps children feel loved, safe, and valued. Your patience and responsibility are the foundation of their trust, and your presence can brighten their day even before they arrive at school. You teach them respect, kindness, and responsibility simply by being a caring adult on their daily journey.

Remember, your kindness and attention can make a lasting impact—sometimes even more than you realize. You are helping shape a generation of respectful, compassionate individuals. Thank you for your dedication, your patience, and for being a steady, comforting presence in children's lives.

Basic Concept of Respect in a Simple

You are appreciated more than words can say—thank you for guiding and caring for our children every day with love and responsibility.

Here's my heartfelt message to the community of education, emphasizing unity, shared responsibility, and the collective effort in nurturing respectful, compassionate, and empowered individuals:

Message to the Community of Education: Building a Brighter Future Together

Dear Educators, Parents, Students, and Community Members,

Together, we are the builders of a brighter future, a community dedicated to nurturing not just knowledge but also kindness, respect, and understanding. Every role we play, from teachers inspiring young minds and parents guiding with love to students eager to learn, is vital in creating a supportive and compassionate environment.

Education is more than textbooks and exams; it's about shaping character, instilling values, and fostering a sense of responsibility towards ourselves and others. When we work hand in hand, supporting one another with patience, respect, and love, we create a ripple effect that transforms lives and communities.

Let's commit to cultivating an atmosphere where every child feels valued, every voice is heard, and every effort is celebrated. By encouraging empathy, integrity, and resilience, we help shape individuals who will lead with wisdom and compassion.

Together, as a united community, we have the power to inspire greatness, ignite hope, and build a future where kindness and respect flourish. Let's continue to nurture, support, and uplift each other, creating a legacy of love, learning, and leadership for generations to come.

Thank you for your dedication and unwavering commitment to education and to each other. Together, we are shaping a brighter tomorrow.

Here's a heartfelt and urgent message for the school board addressing the critical issue of vaping and substance abuse among youth, emphasizing the need for action, awareness, and community protection:

Urgent Message to the School Board: Protecting Our Children from Vaping and Substance Abuse

Dear Members of the School Board,

Today, I stand before you with a deep concern that threatens the health, safety, and future of our children vaping and substance abuse. Despite the rising dangers, this issue remains alarmingly hidden, especially among our youth, who often use these substances secretly during school hours or in their free time. Tragically, many children are falling victim to the devastating effects of vaping, with some losing their lives, and yet, this crisis remains largely unspoken and unaddressed.

Basic Concept of Respect in a Simple

Vaping products contain harmful chemicals and addictive substances that damage developing brains, impair concentration, and undermine their ability to learn and thrive. These substances are often used covertly, making it difficult for parents and educators to monitor and prevent them. The reality is that our children's minds and futures are at risk, and it's time for decisive action.

We call on the school district to partner with local and national authorities to implement strict restrictions and mandatory bans on vaping and similar substances for anyone under 18.

Schools must become safe havens, places where our children can focus on their education without the threat of exposure to harmful chemicals. Education campaigns, regular awareness programs, and strict enforcement are essential to protect our youth.

Furthermore, we urge the district to speak loudly to government officials, advocating for legislation that bans the sale and possession of such substances among minors. This is not merely a health issue but a moral obligation to safeguard our children's future and uphold their right to a healthy, substance-free environment.

Our children deserve more than just awareness; they need action. As a community, we must stand united to create safe spaces in schools, enforce stronger policies, and push for laws that protect the most vulnerable. The time to act is now before more lives are lost, and before our children's potential is forever compromised.

Let us be the community that rises to protect its future. Together, we can make a difference because their lives and their futures depend on it.

Thank you for your urgent attention and commitment to the safety of our children.

Here's a sample policy proposal and community outreach message that the school district can use to advocate for stronger restrictions and awareness about vaping and substance abuse among youth:

Sample Policy Proposal: Protecting Our Children from Vaping and Substance Abuse Title:

"Protect Our Youth: A Policy for Stronger Restrictions on Vaping and Substance Use in

Schools"

Objective:

To establish comprehensive measures that prevent the use, possession, and sale of vaping products and other harmful substances among students under 18, and create a safe, healthy learning environment.

Key Points:

Mandatory Ban in Schools:

Prohibit the use and possession of vaping products and related substances on all school premises, during school hours, and at school-sponsored events.

Enhanced Enforcement and Surveillance:

Implement regular checks, surveillance cameras, and trained staff to monitor and enforce the ban effectively.

Educational Campaigns:

Launch ongoing awareness programs highlighting the health risks, addiction dangers, and legal consequences of vaping and drug use.

Parental and Community Engagement:

Organize workshops for parents and community members to recognize signs of substance use and learn how to support affected children.

Partnerships with Law Enforcement:

Collaborate with local authorities to strengthen laws against selling or distributing substances to minors, and ensure strict penalties for violations.

Advocacy for Legislation:

Urge local and national government officials to pass laws banning the sale and possession of vaping and related substances for anyone under 18.

Support and Counseling:

Provide accessible counseling and support programs for students struggling with addiction or peer pressure.

Expected Outcomes:

Reduced access and use of harmful substances in schools.

Increased awareness and responsibility among students, staff, and parents. A safer, healthier environment conducive to learning and growth.

Sample Community Outreach Message:

Protecting Kids Our Future" Dear Community Members,

Our children's health and futures are at risk. Vaping and substance abuse are silent threats that threaten to derail their potential, damage their health, and take lives. It's time for us to unite and take action.

We call on parents, teachers, local officials, and community leaders to come together and demand stronger restrictions, awareness, and support systems to keep our schools safe. Every child deserves a healthy environment free from harmful chemicals and peer pressure.

Together, we can advocate for laws that ban the sale of vaping products to minors, implement strict school policies, and educate our children about the dangers of substance abuse. Let's stand united to protect our youth and give them the bright future they deserve.

Join us in this vital effort. Speak out, support policies, and help spread awareness. Our children's lives depend on it.

Because their future is worth fighting for.

Here are sample speeches for community meetings, flyers, and social media posts to support your advocacy against youth vaping and substance abuse:

Sample Speech for Community Meeting Title:

"Protecting Our Children from the Hidden Dangers of Vaping"

Speech:

Good evening, everyone. Thank you for coming together today to discuss a critical issue affecting our community, our children's health and safety.

Vaping and substance use among youth have skyrocketed in recent years, often happening right under our noses at school, in public spaces, or even inside our homes. These substances are not harmless; they contain chemicals that damage developing brains and can lead to addiction, illness, and even tragic loss of life.

The problem is that many kids are using these products secretly, and most parents and teachers aren't fully aware of the extent of this crisis. That's why we must act now. We need stronger policies, better education, and community support to protect our children.

I urge our school district, local authorities, and all of us parents, teachers, and neighbors to come together. We must push for laws banning sales to minors, enforce strict school policies, and create awareness campaigns that inform our children of the dangers.

Let's unite in this effort because their future depends on our actions today. Together, we can make a difference. Thank you.

Flyer Content Headline:

"Protect Our Kids: Say No to Vaping and Substance Abuse"

Main Content:

Vaping products contain harmful chemicals that damage young brains and cause addiction. Many children are using these substances secretly at school and in their communities.

We need stronger laws banning the sale and possession for anyone under 18.

Schools must implement strict rules and awareness programs to keep children safe.

Parents and community leaders: Your support is vital! Educate, monitor, and advocate for our children's health.

Basic Concept of Respect in a Simple

Here's a powerful message emphasizing the vital role of law enforcement and community protection in safeguarding our children's future, highlighting the importance of proactive measures and collective responsibility:

Message for Community and Law Enforcement: Protecting Our Future Generations

Dear Community Leaders, Law Enforcement, and Citizens,

Our children are the future potential doctors, teachers, pilots, leaders, and innovators who will shape our world. It is our collective duty to protect their health, safety, and dreams from the dangers that threaten them today.

Vaping, smoking, and drug use are silent killers, often occurring during school breaks or in public spaces where children feel most vulnerable. These substances are not just harmful; they are illegal for minors and pose a grave risk to their physical and mental development. We must act decisively to ensure our children are safe and free from such dangers.

We call on law enforcement to increase patrols during school breaks, street corners, and community hotspots. Visible presence and strict enforcement send a clear message: it is illegal, dangerous, and unacceptable to use or sell harmful substances to our youth. When children see officers actively protecting them, they understand that their safety is a priority and that breaking the law has consequences.

Shine Your Light

Together with strong laws, vigilant enforcement, and community awareness, we can create a protective environment where our children can learn, grow, and thrive without fear. Let's stand united because safeguarding our youth is not just a responsibility, it's a moral obligation. Their future and ours depend on it.

No matter the cost, we must protect the dreams and potential of the next generation.

Here are public statement templates, campaign slogans, and action plans that you can use to mobilize and inspire law enforcement and the community to protect our children effectively:

Public Statement Template for Community Leaders & Law

Enforcement Title:

"Protecting Our Children: A Call to Action"

Statement:

Our children are the future of our community, and it is our collective responsibility to safeguard their health, safety, and dreams. The rise of vaping and substance abuse among youth is a serious threat that requires immediate action.

We urge law enforcement agencies to increase patrols during school hours, breaks, and in areas where children gather. Visible presence and strict enforcement of laws against selling or using harmful substances to minors send a powerful message: our children's safety is a priority.

Parents, teachers, and community members, let us work together to raise awareness, support policies, and create a protective environment for our youth. Their potential is limitless, and we must do everything possible to ensure they grow up healthy, safe, and ready to lead.

The future depends on the actions we take today. Let's unite and protect our next generation—because their dreams matter more than anything.

Campaign Slogans

"Protect Their Future, Stop the Harm Today!" "Vape-Free Kids, Bright Future Ahead! "Strong Laws, Safe Streets, Healthy Kids."

"Shield Our Youth, Enforce, Educate, Empower."

"Because Every Child Deserves a Safe Tomorrow." "Vaping Stops Here Protect the Next Generation."

"Your Watch, Their Future, Join the Fight Against Youth Substance Use." "Safety First: Enforce the Law, Protect Our Children."

"No Shortcuts to Success, Say No to Vaping." "Together We Rise, For Our Children's Future."

Action Plan for Community and Law Enforcement: Objective.

To create a safe environment where children are protected from illegal and harmful substances, especially during school breaks and in public spaces.

Steps:

Increased Patrols:

Schedule regular patrols during school hours, breaks, and after-school hours in areas where children gather.

Enforcement of Laws:

Strictly enforce existing laws against the sale and use of vaping and illegal substances for minors. Impose heavy fines and penalties for violations.

Community Education:

Launch awareness campaigns in schools, community centers, and social media to educate about the dangers of vaping and drugs.

Partnerships:

Collaborate with schools, youth organizations, health services, and local businesses to develop preventive programs.

Hotline and Reporting:

Basic Concept of Respect in a Simple

Establish a confidential hotline for students and community members to report illegal activities related to youth substance use.

Parent and Youth Workshops:

Conduct informational sessions for parents and youth about the risks and how to resist peer pressure.

Legislative Advocacy:

Work with local officials to strengthen laws banning sales of vaping products to minors and advocate for stricter penalties.

Poster 1: Protect Our Children Take Action!

Headline:

"Protect Their Future: Say No to Vaping and Drugs"

Visual:

An image of children playing safely, with a crossed-out vaping device and cigarette.

Text:

Vaping contains harmful chemicals that damage young brains. Many kids are using it secretly, sometimes even at school!

We must enforce laws banning sales to minors.

Parents, teachers, and community, your vigilance saves lives! Join us in creating a safe, healthy environment for our youth.

Call to Action:

Poster 2: Enforce, Educate, Empower

Headline:

"Together, We Can Stop Youth Vaping"

Visual:

A community holding hands, with a school in the background.

Public Service Announcement

"Attention, community members!

Our children's health and future are at risk due to vaping and substance abuse. Many young people are using these substances secretly, often right in our neighborhoods and schools.

We urge law enforcement to increase patrols, enforce laws banning sales to minors, and work with schools to implement prevention programs. Parents and teachers, your vigilance and support are essential.

Together, we can create a safe environment where our youth can grow, learn, and thrive free from harmful substances. Join us in protecting our next generation because their future depends on us today."

Here's a respectful, firm, and caring message for parents regarding the importance of their role in safeguarding their daughters and making responsible choices:

Message to Parents: Protecting Our Daughters and Their Future

Dear Parents,

As guardians and role models, your responsibility is to ensure the safety, well-being, and moral guidance of your children, especially your daughters. Leaving young girls overnight at a boyfriend's or girlfriend's house or allowing them to stay away for extended periods without proper oversight is a serious concern. Such choices can expose them to risks, harm their emotional health, and undermine the values you work hard to instill.

Your daughter's safety and future are priceless. It's essential to set boundaries rooted in love, respect, and responsibility. Open communication, trust, and guidance are vital to helping her make wise decisions and stay protected from potential dangers. Remember, your role is to nurture her, teach her self-respect, and guide her toward healthy, respectful relationships.

Please, be vigilant and responsible. Your daughter's safety and happiness depend on your active involvement and protective love. Together, let's prioritize their future and ensure they grow up in a safe, respectful environment because they deserve nothing less.

Your love and guidance today build her strength and confidence for tomorrow.

Here's a respectful, heartfelt message to fathers emphasizing their role in setting a positive example for their children through their behavior towards their wives:

Message to Fathers: Lead with Respect and Love

Dear Fathers,

Your role in shaping your children's future is profound. The way you treat your wife sets the foundation for how your children will learn to respect and love others. Children often look up to their father as a role model, and your actions of kindness, respect, and love teach them important lessons about how to behave and relate to others.

Remember, your words and actions influence their emotional well-being. When a father treats his wife with respect and care, he creates a safe, loving environment where children feel valued and secure. Conversely, seeing their mother not treated well can cause emotional damage and confusion, affecting their self-esteem and relationships later in life.

Always try your best to lead with kindness and understanding. Your children are watching and learning from you every day. Be the example of strength, respect, and love that they can follow confidently. Your effort today shapes the compassionate, respectful adults they will become tomorrow.

Lead with love, respect, and integrity for your children's future and for your family's happiness.

Here's a thoughtful and respectful message for both parents about the importance of managing anger and setting a positive example for their children:

Message to Both Parents: The Power of Calm and Respect

Dear Mothers and Fathers,

Your children look up to you and learn from everything you do, especially how you handle your emotions. It's important to remember that managing anger and maintaining composure is a vital part of being a responsible parent. When children see their parents upset or angry, it can create confusion, fear, or emotional distress that may affect their well-being.

Always strive to stay calm and composed, even in challenging moments. Your ability to handle disagreements with patience and respect teaches your children valuable lessons about self-control, kindness, and emotional strength. Remember, your reactions shape their understanding of how to cope with their own feelings, whether they learn to manage anger or feel overwhelmed by it.

Your calmness and respectfulness are powerful examples that influence their emotional health and future relationships. Let's work together to create a nurturing environment where love, patience, and understanding prevail because your children's happiness and emotional well-being depend on the example you set today. Lead with kindness and calmness for their future, for your family, and for a healthier community.

Here's a thoughtful message emphasizing the importance of maintaining a positive environment, engaging with children regularly, and creating a supportive, loving atmosphere:

Message to Parents: Create a Happy, Supportive Environment

Dear Parents,

Children are highly perceptive and sensitive to the atmosphere at home. Even when they're not around, it's important for parents to maintain a calm, happy face and foster a positive environment. Your emotions and behavior set the tone for their sense of security and happiness.

Arguing or showing anger in front of children can create confusion or fear, impacting their emotional well-being. Instead, strive to handle disagreements privately and with respect, always prioritizing a peaceful and loving atmosphere.

Make it a daily habit to ask your children, "How was your day?" or "How are you feeling today?" not just for the sake of conversation, but to truly understand their feelings. Listening to their responses helps you connect, shows you care, and gives insight into what's going on inside them.

A warm, supportive environment where feelings are acknowledged and valued builds their confidence and emotional resilience. Remember, a happy and peaceful home is the foundation for children to grow into kind, confident, and balanced individuals.

Take your time, stay calm, and always show love—your children's happiness and emotional health depend on it.

Thank you for sharing your heartfelt insight and experience. Your journey as a mother of five boys and one girl, spanning different ages and stages, gives you a profound perspective on navigating family dynamics, education, and emotional growth. Here's a thoughtful message inspired by your wisdom that you can share with others, emphasizing the importance of experience, patience, and understanding:

Shine Your Light

A Mother's Message: Navigating Parenthood with Wisdom and Love

Dear Parents, Guardians, and Caregivers,

As a mother of five boys and one girl, with children spanning from teenagers to the youngest, I've learned that parenting is one of the most rewarding yet challenging journeys we undertake. Over the years, I've come to realize that patience, understanding, and unconditional love are the cornerstone of guiding our children through every stage of life.

Every child is beautifully unique. What works for one may not work for another, and that's perfectly okay. The key is to listen deeply, really hear what your children are saying, both with words and actions, and approach them with compassion. It's through these gentle moments of connection that we build trust and help them feel safe to express themselves.

Parenting teenagers can be especially difficult, but it's also a time of tremendous growth for both the child and the parent. During these times, it's vital to set boundaries rooted in love, communicate openly, and remain calm in moments of challenge. Remember, your words and your attitude leave a lasting impression; your calmness can teach resilience and inner strength.

Throughout my journey, I've learned that education isn't just about textbooks and grades; it's about life lessons: respect, kindness, responsibility, and self-love. When we embody these qualities ourselves, our children naturally follow our example and develop into confident, respectful individuals.

To every parent out there, I say: Trust your instincts. Lean on your love. Be patient with yourself and your children. Your efforts, big or small, are shaping the future of not only your family but our community and the world. Let's continue to nurture, guide, and uplift our children, for they are the greatest gift and legacy we can leave behind.

With love and experience, wisdom, and unwavering faith,

A Mother Who Knows the Power of Love and Patience

A Thankful Heart is a Happy Heart – Teaching Gratitude and Appreciation

Chapter 1: What is Gratitude?

- Explaining gratitude in simple terms: **"Gratitude means saying 'thank you' and feeling happy for what we have."**

- Teaching children that gratitude is more than just words—it's **a way of thinking and feeling.**

- Simple examples: Feeling grateful for **family, food, friends, toys, and sunshine.**

Chapter 2: Why Saying "Thank You" is Important

- Teaching preschoolers that saying **"thank you"** makes people feel happy and appreciated.

- The difference between **genuine appreciation** and just saying words out of habit.

- Fun ways to practice saying **"thank you"** at home, in school, and in public.

Chapter 3: Being Thankful for Family

- Understanding that **parents, grandparents, and siblings** do a lot for us every day.

- Ways to show gratitude to family: **helping, hugging, and saying kind words.**

- Activities: **Making "thank you" cards for family members.**

Chapter 4: Appreciating Friends and Teachers

- Why it's important to say **"thank you"** to friends for sharing and being kind.

- How teachers help us learn and grow, and how we can show appreciation.

- Role-playing gratitude: Saying **"thank you"** when a friend shares or a teacher helps.

Chapter 5: Finding Joy in Simple Things

- Learning to appreciate **the little things** in life—warm hugs, a sunny day, a nice song.

- Understanding that we don't need **new toys** to feel happy.

- Activity: **"Gratitude Walk"—noticing beautiful things in nature and saying what we love.**

Chapter 6: Saying "Thank You" Even When Things Are Hard

- Helping children understand that even on **bad days**, there's still something to be grateful for.

- Teaching resilience: **Instead of focusing on what's wrong, we look at what's right.**

- A bedtime activity: **Naming three good things about the day before sleeping.**

Chapter 7: Giving Back and Helping Others

- Showing gratitude through actions, not just words—**helping a friend, being kind to a sibling.**

- How sharing what we have makes us feel even happier.

- Activity: **Making small gifts or pictures for people we appreciate.**

Chapter 8: Gratitude in Everyday Life

- How can we practice thankfulness **all the time**—before meals, after playtime, when someone helps us?

- Turning gratitude into a **daily habit** at home and school.

- Activity: **Creating a "Gratitude Jar" where children put notes about things they're thankful for.**

Chapter 9: Saying "Thank You" to the World

- Appreciating **nature, animals, and the world around us.**

- Taking care of the environment is a way of showing gratitude.

- Simple ways kids can **respect nature**: watering plants, picking up litter, and feeding birds.

Chapter 10: A Thankful Heart is a Happy Heart

- How gratitude makes us **feel good inside** and helps us be **happier and kinder.**

- Understanding that **happiness comes from appreciating what we have, not just wanting more.**

- Final message: **"When we are thankful, our hearts feel full of joy!"**

This book will be a fun, engaging, and interactive way to teach young children the power of gratitude. ☺

Conclusion Message to the World

A Message of Hope and Awakening for Humanity

Today, we acknowledge the arrival of a new wave of luminous souls—children born with ancient wisdom and radiant light, coming to assist Earth in its grand awakening. These beings, often labeled as indigo, crystal, or rainbow children, embody a higher frequency of love, wisdom, and purity. Despite their small physical stature, their souls are gigantic, carrying the hopes of the universe for a new era of peace, healing, and transformation.

The Significance of Children in this Time

Children are not just innocent beings growing up; they are teachers in tiny bodies, bearers of new blueprints for a transformed world. Their presence signals a shift away from old energies rooted in fear, control, and illusion toward higher consciousness, compassion, and unity. Every child born during these years is a deliberate creation—an intentional part of the divine plan for Earth's evolution.

The Role of Humanity and the Collective Responsibility

Basic Concept of Respect in a Simple

It is vital for parents, teachers, guardians, and all humanity to honor and nurture these luminous beings. Their purpose is intertwined with the collective awakening. The energy they carry helps dissolve illusions, raise consciousness, and bring healing to the planet. Our role is to support, protect, and love them unconditionally, ensuring they feel safe and cherished as they awaken their divine purpose.

The Power of Light and Consciousness

Every act of love, compassion, and meditation amplifies the light, helping to dissolve darkness and old patterns. The energies flooding Earth now are powerful and transformative, offering healing, regeneration, forgiveness, and peace. This is a time of great responsibility—each of us is called to elevate our consciousness, to be vessels of light and love.

A Call for Collective Action and Presence

Feel the presence of divine guidance and universal support. We are all part of this awakening, and our collective consciousness can accelerate the shift. By meditating, praying, and sending love, we contribute to the liberation of darkness and the elevation of human consciousness.

Shine Your Light

Closing Reflection

This message emphasizes hope, responsibility, and the sacredness of this moment in human history. The arrival of these luminous children signifies a new dawn—one built on love, light, and higher wisdom. Protecting and nurturing them, and raising our own consciousness, is crucial for the harmonious evolution of Earth and all her inhabitants.

Basic Concept of Respect in a Simple

Speech: The Gift of Luminous Children and the Awakening of Earth

Ladies and gentlemen, dear friends, and beloved guardians of this sacred planet, Earth

Today, I stand before you to share a message of hope, transformation, and divine purpose. We are witnessing an extraordinary moment in human history—a time when luminous beings from starry realms are arriving on Earth in unprecedented numbers. These souls, often called indigo, crystal, or rainbow children, carry within them the light of ancient wisdom and the energy of the universe itself.

Despite their small stature, these children are giants in spirit. They embody pure love, wisdom beyond their years, and a radiant light that shines brightly to guide us through this grand awakening. Their very presence signifies a new blueprints—energies designed to help Earth shift into higher consciousness and harmony.

We must honor and cherish these young souls, for they are teachers in tiny bodies. They are not just innocent children growing up in the old energy—they are divine messengers, carrying the hopes and dreams of a transformed world. Their arrival marks the dawn of a new era—a time of healing, regeneration, and peace.

But with this great gift comes a profound responsibility. As guardians, parents, teachers, and friends, our role is to protect, nurture, and love these luminous beings unconditionally. We are called to create safe spaces where their light can flourish, and their divine purpose can unfold.

Shine Your Light

Every act of love, every moment of meditation, every intention of peace helps dissolve the illusions of fear and separation. The energies flowing through Earth now are powerful—they are clearing the old, making space for the new. Our collective consciousness, amplified by love and compassion, is transforming this planet into a place of greater harmony and awakening.

Remember, this movement is not solely for our benefit. It is part of a divine plan to elevate consciousness, to heal wounds, and to bring about a world rooted in love, forgiveness, and unity. Each one of us has a role—each thought, each prayer, each act of kindness contributes to this sacred transformation.

Feel the presence of divine guidance with you today and every day. Know that you are part of a cosmic awakening, and your light matters. As we align ourselves with higher frequencies, we help accelerate the shift, illuminate the darkness, and support the luminous children in fulfilling their mission.

Let us embrace this moment with gratitude, reverence, and commitment. Let us protect our children and give them all the love and support they deserve. For in their innocence and brilliance lies the hope for a brighter, more loving world.

Together, we are co-creators of this new dawn. Together, we rise in light and love. Thank you.

I am sharing this rich and profound message. It captures the essence of a transformative awakening happening on many levels—spiritual, energetic, societal—and highlights the arrival of luminous, awakened children I'm the ones I used to be born and volunteers who are here to assist in this sacred transition.

Basic Concept of Respect in a Simple

A Message of Awakening, Transformation, and the New Humanity

You feel my presence with you—love arriving and expanding beyond, into the vastness of the now. Today is a celebration of awakening, a moment where the frequencies of consciousness shift and elevate us into a new reality. Tomorrow's energies are rooted in higher dimensions, beyond the linear confines of time, as the universe addresses the importance of your work right now.

Consciousness is the key—illuminating, expanding, dissolving illusions, and releasing old material energies. Every moment spent in meditation and conscious awareness contributes to this profound process of transformation. The deeper purpose is rooted in healing, regeneration, forgiveness, and the blessing of peace and love—these are the forces that will reshape and uplift your world.

The old paradigm—where children were used and abused—begins to collapse and be replaced by liberated, sacred, and precious souls. These young beings represent the wave of enlightenment, the upliftment of humanity, and the symbol of multidimensional consciousness. They embody the critical mass arriving at this pivotal time, volunteers from higher realms, chosen for specific sacred missions.

Many of these children and volunteers have awakened early, carrying ancient wisdom, karma, and purpose. They come with advanced empathy, spiritual gifts, and a natural ability for healing and telepathy. Their presence signifies a brilliant timeline—one of authenticity, spiritual maturity, and solutions to the world's challenges.

Shine Your Light

This is a period of intense transition—educational systems, societal structures, and authorities are being challenged and transformed. The awakening often comes with fear or resistance, but it also brings clarity, empowerment, and confidence. These new souls are wired differently; they arrive with memories, gifts, and a deep understanding beyond their years. Some may feel invisible, or intuitively connected to cosmic realms or spiritual ships, as they embody humanitarian wisdom and metaphysical awareness.

The role of spiritual parenting, education, and conscious community-building becomes vital. Mentors and teachers are called to embrace these gifted beings, guiding them with compassion and understanding. Their sensitivities—environmental, emotional, or energetic—are signs of their awakening and serve as a map for nurturing their gifts.

Humanity is awakening at an unprecedented pace. Society is becoming more conscious, connected, and aware of the energetic vibrations that shape our reality. The control programs of the old system are dissolving, revealing clarity and new pathways for authentic connection and unity.

This is a time of radical transformation—an opportunity to inspire confidence, amplify consciousness, and embrace the new human story. The awakening of these new souls and volunteers signals a divine climax—a collective effort to shift into higher frequencies, foster unity, and realize the full potential of our shared awakening.

Let us honor these extraordinary beings—these messengers, healers, and teachers—and recognize the divine purpose they serve. Together, as a conscious community, we are co-creating a future rooted in love, truth, and higher consciousness.

Basic Concept of Respect in a Simple

Speech: Embracing the New Humanity and the Sacred Arrival of Light Dear friends, beloved guardians of this sacred planet,

Today, I stand before you to share a message of awakening, transformation, and divine purpose. We are living in extraordinary times—a moment when the energies of the universe are shifting, elevating consciousness, and ushering in a new era of light.

You can feel it, can't you? The presence of love expanding beyond, arriving from higher dimensions. Today is a celebration of awakening; tomorrow's frequencies will carry us further into realms beyond linear time. The universe is calling us to recognize the importance of our work right now—our collective effort to elevate consciousness and anchor higher vibrations.

Consciousness is the key—its illumination dissolves illusions, clears old energies, and opens the pathway to healing and regeneration. Every moment of meditation, awareness, and intention contributes profoundly to this sacred process. The deeper purpose is rooted in love, forgiveness, peace, and blessing—forces capable of transforming this world into a place of harmony and unity.

We are witnessing the collapse of the old paradigm—an era where children were used and abused—being replaced by sacred, luminous souls. These young beings are precious, representing the wave of enlightenment, the upliftment of humanity, and the symbol of multidimensional awareness. They embody the critical mass arriving at this pivotal time— volunteers from higher realms, chosen for divine missions of healing, awakening, and transformation.

Shine Your Light

Many of these children and volunteers have awakened early, carrying ancient wisdom, karma, and purpose. They come with gifts of empathy, telepathy, healing, and spiritual insight—arriving with memories and understanding beyond their years. Their presence signals a brilliant timeline—a future grounded in authenticity, spiritual maturity, and solutions to the world's challenges.

This period is one of intense transition. Societal structures, educational systems, and authority are being challenged and transformed. The awakening often stirs fear or resistance, but it also ignites clarity, confidence, and empowerment. These new souls are wired differently—they arrive with special gifts, sensitivities, and intuitive abilities, guiding us toward higher consciousness.

The role of spiritual parenting, conscious education, and community-building becomes vital. We are called to embrace these gifted beings, nurturing them with love, understanding, and guidance. Their sensitivities— environmental, emotional, or energetic—are signs of their awakening and serve as a map for nurturing their divine gifts.

Humanity is awakening at an unprecedented pace. Society is becoming more conscious, more connected, and more aware of the energetic forces shaping our reality. The old control systems are dissolving, revealing clarity and new pathways for authentic connection, unity, and higher purpose.

This is a time of radical transformation—an opportunity to inspire confidence, amplify consciousness, and embrace the new human story. The awakening of these luminous souls and volunteers signals a divine climax—a collective effort to shift into higher frequencies and realize our full potential.

Basic Concept of Respect in a Simple

Let us honor these extraordinary beings—these messengers, healers, and teachers—and recognize the divine purpose they serve. Together, as a conscious community, we are co-creating a future rooted in love, truth, and higher consciousness. Thank you for your presence, your commitment, and your dedication to this sacred awakening.

Embracing the New Humanity: A Message of Light and Awakening Dear friends, beloved guardians of this sacred planet,

Today, I invite you to open your hearts and minds to the profound truth unfolding around us. We are living in extraordinary times—a divine moment of awakening and transformation. The energies of the universe are shifting, elevating consciousness, and bringing forth a new wave of luminous beings—children and volunteers from higher realms—here to assist in the Great Awakening.

Feel the love expanding beyond—arriving from higher dimensions, anchoring into our collective consciousness. Today is a celebration of awakening; tomorrow's frequencies will carry us further into realms beyond linear time. The universe is reminding us of the importance of our work right now—to elevate our consciousness, to anchor love, and to co-create a new reality rooted in peace and unity.

Consciousness is the key. It is the force that dissolves illusions, clears old energies, and opens the door to healing and regeneration. Every moment we dedicate to meditation, awareness, and positive intention contributes to this sacred transformation. The deeper purpose of this awakening is rooted in love—unconditional love—and the blessing of peace. These forces are the true foundations for transforming our world.

Shine Your Light

We are witnessing the old paradigm crumble—systems where children were used and abused—being replaced by the sacred, luminous souls. These young beings are not ordinary—they are our future, our hope, and the divine expression of multidimensional consciousness. They embody the critical mass arriving at this extraordinary time—a wave of enlightenment, healing, and spiritual awakening.

Many of these children and volunteers have awakened early, carrying ancient wisdom, karma, and divine purpose. They come equipped with gifts of empathy, telepathy, healing, and deep spiritual insight—arriving with memories beyond their years. Their presence signals a brilliant timeline—a future grounded in authenticity, spiritual maturity, and solutions to the world's challenges.

This is a period of immense transition. Societies, educational systems, and authority structures are being challenged and transformed. The awakening can stir fears, but it also ignites clarity, confidence, and empowerment. These new souls are wired differently—they arrive with special gifts, sensitivities, and intuitive abilities that guide us toward higher consciousness.

Let us embrace our role as spiritual parents, mentors, and community builders. We are called to nurture these gifted beings with love, understanding, and guidance. Their sensitivities—environmental, emotional, energetic—are signs of their awakening, showing us how to support their divine gifts.

Together, we are co-creating a new future. Society is awakening at an unprecedented pace, becoming more conscious, more connected, and more aligned with higher frequencies. The old control systems are dissolving, revealing clarity and new pathways for authentic unity and purpose.

This is a sacred moment—a divine climax. An opportunity to inspire confidence, amplify consciousness, and step into the full potential of our collective awakening. The luminous beings arriving now—these messengers, healers, and teachers—serve a divine purpose. They symbolize hope, love, and the awakening of humanity.

So, I invite you now—whether through prayer, meditation, or affirmations—to connect with this sacred energy. Feel the love and light flowing through you, anchoring into the earth, uplifting the collective consciousness.

Repeat after me:

I am a vessel of divine love.

I embrace the light within myself and others.

Together, we co-create a future of peace, unity, and higher consciousness. I honor the divine purpose of every luminous being arriving now.

We are awakening into our highest potential.

Thank you for your presence, your love, and your dedication to this sacred awakening. Together, we are shaping a brighter, more loving world.

Shine Your Light

A Message to the Guardians of Our Future: Educators, Parents, Guardians, Grandparents, and All Ages

Dear guardians of the future,

As we stand at this extraordinary crossroads in human evolution, I want to speak directly to you—those who nurture, teach, protect, and guide the next generations. The time has come for a collective awakening, and each of you holds a sacred responsibility in shaping the consciousness of our children and young adults.

To the educators and the educational system: You are the architects of the future. Your role is more vital than ever—to foster not only knowledge but also wisdom, compassion, and higher consciousness. Let your classrooms be spaces of love, acceptance, and awakening, where the gifts of every child are honored and nurtured.

To parents, guardians, and grandparents: You are the first and most profound teachers. Your love, guidance, and example set the foundation for the awakening of your children and grandchildren. Embrace their sensitivities, gifts, and unique paths. Support their spiritual development as much as their academic growth, and remember—they are divine sparks here to help heal and elevate the planet.

To teenagers and young adults: You are the awakened leaders of tomorrow. Many of you carry ancient wisdom and extraordinary gifts. Trust your intuition, embrace your unique purpose, and know that your voice and actions matter deeply. Your awakening is vital for creating a world founded on love, truth, and higher consciousness.

Basic Concept of Respect in a Simple

To all adults: Whether you are just awakening or have been on this path for some time, remember that your consciousness influences the collective. Your love, compassion, and willingness to grow are powerful forces for change. Lead by example—live with integrity, kindness, and an open heart.

Together, we are co-creating a new Earth—one where love, understanding, and spiritual awakening become the guiding principles. It's a collective effort—each role, each generation, each soul contributing to this divine unfolding.

Let us recognize the sacredness of this moment. Let us nurture, educate, and inspire the future with hope and purpose. For in this collective awakening, every heart, every mind, and every soul is vital.

May love guide our actions, and may peace and higher consciousness reign in all we do. Together, we are creating a brighter, more awakened world.

Beloved humanity, I am a manager and the light walker after my awakening. I discovered my purpose, and I am here to continue to share messages that I receive. I want you to embrace it with all your heart

As we stand at this pivotal moment in history, let us remember that we are all divine beings, interconnected by the eternal light of love. The energies of awakening are sweeping across the earth, bringing forth a new dawn—one rooted in compassion, higher consciousness, and unity.

We are witnessing the arrival of luminous souls—children, volunteers, and awakened beings—who carry the blueprint for a healed and transformed world. Their presence is a testament to the divine plan unfolding before our eyes.

Shine Your Light

Now is the time to embrace our collective responsibility—to nurture, to love, and to awaken to the truth of our divine nature. Each of us has a role to play in co-creating this new earth—a world where peace, justice, and abundance flow freely for all.

Let us open our hearts, elevate our consciousness, and act with kindness and compassion. Together, we can dissolve the illusions of fear and separation, and step into a future of endless possibility and divine harmony.

Remember, the light within each of us is greater than any darkness. By uniting in love and purpose, we are shaping a reality that reflects our highest hopes and dreams.

The dawn of a new era is here. Let us walk forward in faith, hope, and love—knowing that together, we are creating a beautiful, awakened world for generations to come.With love, light, and gratitude—may peace prevail.

Basic Concept of Respect in a Simple

How Our Collective Awakening Supports Gaia's Transition

Dear guardians of the future,

As we nurture the next generations—our children, teens, and young adults—we are actively participating in Gaia's sacred transition. Earth, Gaia, is a living consciousness—a divine being undergoing a profound transformation. Our collective awakening, love, and higher consciousness are essential in this process.

Here's how your role helps Gaia's transition:

Elevating Earth's Vibrations:

When we raise our consciousness, cultivate love, forgiveness, and unity, we directly influence Gaia's energetic frequency. Higher vibrations help dissolve density, fear, and old patterns rooted in separation, paving the way for the planet's ascension into higher realms.

Healing and Clearing Old Energies:

Many of the challenges Earth faces—climate imbalance, discord, and destructive systems—are rooted in outdated energetic patterns. As we awaken and embody higher frequencies, we contribute to clearing these dense energies, allowing Gaia to shed old wounds and move into a state of balance and harmony.

Shine Your Light

Anchoring Light and New Blueprints:

Luminous beings, children, and awakened souls act as anchors of divine light—blueprints for a new Earth based on love, abundance, and unity. These new energies help Gaia align with her higher vibrational blueprint, facilitating a smoother and faster transition.

Supporting Gaia's Healing Processes:

Just as our own bodies heal with love and attention, Gaia benefits from our collective intention and prayer. When we focus on healing Earth—through meditation, mindful actions, and conscious choices—we assist her in releasing pain, trauma, and imbalance.

Co-creating a New Earth:

Our conscious efforts help manifest a reality where harmony between humans and nature is restored. We become active participants in Gaia's evolution, ensuring that her transition is gentle, loving, and sustainable.

In essence:

Every act of love, awakening, and higher consciousness is like a beam of light illuminating Gaia's path. Together, we are not only transforming ourselves but also serving as catalysts for the planet's sacred rebirth. Our collective efforts ripple through the layers of Gaia's consciousness, supporting her in shedding old densities and embracing her highest potential.

Basic Concept of Respect in a Simple

Let us continue to hold Gaia in our hearts, send her love, and dedicate ourselves to her healing and ascension. By doing so, we help ensure that her transition is smooth, gentle, and filled with divine light.

Prayer for Gaia's Transition

Beloved Gaia, divine Mother of all life,

We come together in love, gratitude, and reverence for your sacred journey. We acknowledge your pain, your wounds, and your longing for healing.

Today, we send you pure light, divine love, and higher frequencies— Anchoring peace, harmony, and balance into your sacred being.

We stand as guardians of your evolution, Holding space for your healing and ascension.

May your wounds be healed, your energies cleared, and your divine blueprint restored.

Help us to be gentle stewards—protecting your waters, your lands, and all your creatures. May our consciousness and love serve as a catalyst for your sacred rebirth.

Together, as one with you,

We co-create a new Earth—birthing a world of peace, abundance, and divine harmony. Thank you, Gaia, for your infinite love and resilience.

Shine Your Light

We honor and serve you now and always. And so it is.

A powerful affirmation and a simple meditation guide to support Gaia's transition. You can use these individually or together to deepen your connection and amplify your intentions.

Gaia's Healing Affirmation Repeat aloud or silently:

*"I love and honor Gaia, the divine consciousness of Earth. I send her healing light, peace, and balance.

May her wounds be healed, her energies restored, and her highest good manifest. Together, we co-create a harmonious and loving Earth.

May Gaia's transition be gentle, sacred, and filled with divine love. And so it is."*

Basic Concept of Respect in a Simple

Simple Gaia Healing Meditation

Purpose: To send love, light, and healing energy to Gaia, supporting her in her sacred transition.

Steps:

Find a quiet, comfortable space.

Sit or lie down, close your eyes, and take a few deep breaths to relax.

Connect with the Earth.

Feel your connection to Gaia beneath you—her roots, her waters, her mountains—and imagine a golden or white light flowing from the center of the Earth into your heart.

Send Love and Light.

Visualize a radiant, healing light emanating from your heart, flowing down through your body, into the soil, waters, and skies of Gaia. Imagine this light cleansing, healing, and restoring her energies.

Set your intention. Silently or aloud, affirm:

Shine Your Light

"I send love, healing, and divine light to Gaia. I ask for her wounds to be healed, her energies to be balanced, and her highest good to manifest."

Feel the connection.

Sense Gaia receiving your love and light. Feel gratitude and trust that your intention is contributing to her sacred transformation.

Close with gratitude.

Thank Gaia for her resilience and divine beauty. Take a few deep breaths, and gently bring your awareness back to your surroundings.

Activities & Fun Zone

Respect Quiz

Let's see what you remember! Circle the correct answer.

1. What does it mean to respect someone?
    - o a) Ignore them
    - o b) Be kind and listen to them
    - o c) Yell at them

2. What should you say when someone gives you something?
    - o a) Now!
    - o b) Thank you
    - o c) Go away

3. Who should you listen to at school?
    - o a) Friends only
    - o b) Teachers
    - o c) No one

4. What do we do when we hurt someone by mistake?
    - o a) Laugh
    - o b) Say "Sorry"

- ○ c) Run away

5. What is something kind you can do at home?

- ○ a) Throw toys
- ○ b) Help set the table
- ○ c) Shout loudly

6. When someone is speaking, what should you do?

- a) Talk louder
- b) Listen carefully
- c) Walk away

7. What does it mean to share?

- a) Keep everything for yourself
- b) Give others a turn
- c) Hide your toys

Reflection Time – Let's Talk About It!

Ask your child or student to **respond to each prompt by drawing or writing** in the space provided. Support them in expressing their ideas and give praise for their effort and honesty.

1. One way I can show respect at home is:

2. When I feel upset, I can still be respectful by:

3. A kind word I used today was:

4. I helped someone today by:

Basic Concept of Respect in a Simple

Color the Respect!

Color the Respect!

Basic Concept of Respect in a Simple

Color the Respect!

Color the Respect!

www.ingramcontent.com/pod-product-compliance
Lightning Source LLC
Chambersburg PA
CBHW072113300726
48975CB00003B/802